Alice's Adventures In Wonderland

and

Through The Looking Glass

by

Lewis Carroll:

Stacked Prose Edition

Alice's Adventures In Wonderland

and

Through The Looking Glass

by

Lewis Carroll:

Stacked Prose Edition

ADAPTED BY LANCE CARTER

Alice's Adventures in Wonderland and Through the Looking Glass
by Lewis Carroll: Stacked Prose Edition
Adapted by Lance Carlyle Carter

ISBN: 978-1-935057-28-4
Copyright © 2022 by Lance Carlyle Carter

TABLE OF CONTENTS

Alice's Adventures in Wonderland

CHAPTER I.   Down the Rabbit-Hole 1
CHAPTER II.   The Pool of Tears 7
CHAPTER III.   A Caucus-Race and a Long Tale 13
CHAPTER IV.   The Rabbit Sends in a Little Bill 18
CHAPTER V.   Advice from a Caterpillar 25
CHAPTER VI.   Pig and Pepper 31
CHAPTER VII.   A Mad Tea-Party 39
CHAPTER VIII.   The Queen's Croquet-Ground 46
CHAPTER IX.   The Mock Turtle's Story 54
CHAPTER X.   The Lobster Quadrille 61
CHAPTER XI.   Who Stole the Tarts? 68
CHAPTER XII.   Alice's Evidence 74

Through the Looking-Glass, And What Alice Found There

CHAPTER I.   Looking-Glass house 83
CHAPTER II.   The Garden of Live Flowers 92
CHAPTER III.   Looking-Glass Insects 100
CHAPTER IV.   Tweedledum And Tweedledee 109
CHAPTER V.   Wool and Water 119
CHAPTER VI.   Humpty Dumpty 128
CHAPTER VII.   The Lion and the Unicorn 138
CHAPTER VIII.   "It's my own Invention" 146
CHAPTER IX.   Queen Alice 158
CHAPTER X.   Shaking 170
CHAPTER XI.   Waking 170
CHAPTER XII.   Which Dreamed it? 170

INTRODUCTION

These adaptations of *Alice's Adventures In Wonderland* and *Through The Looking-Glass* are faithful to Lewis Carroll's original text except the stories in this edition are in the stacked prose format instead of being boxed in paragraphs.

The pages are divided into two columns of text and the lines are short and often divided by punctuation such as a comma, period, or question mark, which can make for fast and easy reading.

This stacked prose format adaptation breaks up lines of text in the way you would read them aloud and is ideal for speed reading, reading aloud, and dramatic reading.

Empty lines are inserted instead of paragraph indents, as in early editions of these texts. This adaptation makes the story easy to read without the hyphenation of words at the ends of lines. The human eye may get tired reading across a wide line of text, but when lines are short the reading can be faster. The stacked prose format is ideal for young readers, older readers, foreign readers, and new readers. It's time to start reading outside the box!

Lance Carlyle Carter
March 2022

Alice's Adventures In Wonderland

By Lewis Carroll: Stacked Prose Edition

TABLE OF CONTENTS

CHAPTER I. Down the Rabbit-Hole 1
CHAPTER II. The Pool of Tears 7
CHAPTER III. A Caucus-Race and a Long Tale 13
CHAPTER IV. The Rabbit Sends in a Little Bill 18
CHAPTER V. Advice from a Caterpillar 25
CHAPTER VI. Pig and Pepper 31
CHAPTER VII. A Mad Tea-Party 39
CHAPTER VIII. The Queen's Croquet-Ground 46
CHAPTER IX. The Mock Turtle's Story 54
CHAPTER X. The Lobster Quadrille 61
CHAPTER XI. Who Stole the Tarts? 68
CHAPTER XII. Alice's Evidence 74

CHAPTER I.

Down the Rabbit-Hole

Alice was beginning
to get very tired of sitting
by her sister on the bank,
and of having nothing to do:
once or twice she had peeped into
the book her sister was reading,
but it had no pictures
or conversations in it,
"and what is the use of a book,"
thought Alice "without pictures
or conversations?"

So she was considering
in her own mind
(as well as she could,
for the hot day made her feel
very sleepy and stupid),
whether the pleasure
of making a daisy-chain
would be worth the trouble
of getting up
and picking the daisies,
when suddenly a White Rabbit
with pink eyes ran close by her.

There was nothing
so very remarkable in that;
nor did Alice
think it so very much
out of the way
to hear the Rabbit say to itself,
"Oh dear! Oh dear!
I shall be late!"
(when she thought it over
afterwards, it occurred to her
that she ought to have
wondered at this, but at the time
it all seemed quite natural);
but when the Rabbit
actually took a watch

out of its waistcoat-pocket ,
and looked at it,
and then hurried on,
Alice started to her feet,
for it flashed across her mind
that she had never before seen
a rabbit with either
a waistcoat-pocket,
or a watch to take out of it,
and burning with curiosity,
she ran across the field after it,
and fortunately was just in time
to see it pop down
a large rabbit-hole
under the hedge.
In another moment
down went Alice after it,
never once considering
how in the world
she was to get out again.

The rabbit-hole went straight on
like a tunnel for some way,
and then dipped suddenly down,
so suddenly that Alice
had not a moment
to think about stopping herself
before she found herself
falling down a very deep well.

Either the well was very deep,
or she fell very slowly,
for she had plenty of time
as she went down
to look about her and to wonder
what was going to happen next.
First, she tried to look down
and make out what
she was coming to,
but it was too dark
to see anything; then she looked
at the sides of the well,
and noticed that they were filled
with cupboards

and book-shelves;
here and there she saw maps
and pictures hung upon pegs.
She took down a jar from
one of the shelves as she passed;
it was labelled
"ORANGE MARMALADE",
but to her great disappointment
it was empty: she did not like
to drop the jar for fear
of killing somebody underneath,
so managed to put it into one
of the cupboards
as she fell past it.

"Well!" thought Alice to herself,
"after such a fall as this,
I shall think nothing
of tumbling down stairs!
How brave
they'll all think me at home!
Why,
I wouldn't say anything about it,
even if I fell off
the top of the house!"
(Which was very likely true.)

Down, down, down.
Would the fall never come
to an end?
"I wonder how many miles
I've fallen by this time?"
she said aloud.
"I must be getting somewhere
near the centre of the earth.
Let me see:
that would be four thousand
miles down, I think—"
(for, you see,
Alice had learnt several things
of this sort in her lessons
in the schoolroom,
and though this was not
a very good opportunity

for showing off her knowledge,
as there was no one
to listen to her,
still it was good practice
to say it over) "—yes,
that's about the right distance—
but then I wonder what Latitude
or Longitude I've got to?"
(Alice had no idea
what Latitude was,
or Longitude either,
but thought they were
nice grand words to say.)

Presently she began again.
"I wonder if I shall fall
right through the earth!
How funny it'll seem to come out
among the people that walk
with their heads downward!
The Antipathies, I think—"
(she was rather glad
there was no one listening,
this time,
as it didn't sound at all
the right word)
"—but I shall have to ask them
what the name
of the country is, you know.
Please, Ma'am, is this
New Zealand or Australia?"
(and she tried to curtsey
as she spoke—fancy curtseying
as you're falling through the air!
Do you think
you could manage it?)
"And what an ignorant little girl
she'll think me for asking!
No, it'll never do to ask:
perhaps I shall see it
written up somewhere."

Down, down, down.
There was nothing else to do,

so Alice soon began talking again.
"Dinah'll miss me
very much to-night,
I should think!"
(Dinah was the cat.)
"I hope they'll remember her
saucer of milk at tea-time.
Dinah my dear! I wish you were
down here with me!
There are no mice in the air,
I'm afraid,
but you might catch a bat,
and that's very like a mouse,
you know.
But do cats eat bats, I wonder?"
And here Alice
began to get rather sleepy,
and went on saying to herself,
in a dreamy sort of way,
"Do cats eat bats?
Do cats eat bats?" and sometimes,
"Do bats eat cats?" for, you see,
as she couldn't answer
either question,
it didn't much matter
which way she put it.
She felt that she was dozing off,
and had just begun to dream
that she was walking
hand in hand with Dinah,
and saying to her very earnestly,
"Now, Dinah, tell me the truth:
did you ever eat a bat?"
when suddenly, thump! thump!
down she came upon a heap
of sticks and dry leaves,
and the fall was over.

Alice was not a bit hurt,
and she jumped up
on to her feet in a moment:
she looked up,
but it was all dark overhead;
before her was

another long passage,
and the White Rabbit
was still in sight,
hurrying down it.
There was not
a moment to be lost:
away went Alice like the wind,
and was just in time to hear it say,
as it turned a corner,
"Oh my ears and whiskers,
how late it's getting!
" She was close behind it
when she turned the corner,
but the Rabbit
was no longer to be seen:
she found herself in a long,
low hall,
which was lit up by a row
of lamps hanging from the roof.

There were doors
all round the hall,
but they were all locked;
and when Alice
had been all the way down
one side and up the other,
trying every door,
she walked sadly down
the middle,
wondering how she was ever
to get out again.

Suddenly she came upon
a little three-legged table,
all made of solid glass;
there was nothing on it
except a tiny golden key,
and Alice's first thought
was that it might belong
to one of the doors of the hall;
but, alas!
either the locks were too large,
or the key was too small,
but at any rate

it would not open any of them.
However,
on the second time round,
she came upon a low curtain
she had not noticed before,
and behind it was a little door
about fifteen inches high:
she tried the little golden key
in the lock,
and to her great delight it fitted!

Alice opened the door and found
that it led into a small passage,
not much larger than a rat-hole:
she knelt down and looked along
the passage into the loveliest
garden you ever saw.
How she longed to get out
of that dark hall,
and wander about among
those beds of bright flowers
and those cool fountains,
but she could not even
get her head
through the doorway;
"and even if my head
would go through,"
thought poor Alice,
"it would be of very little use
without my shoulders.
Oh, how I wish I could shut up
like a telescope! I think I could,
if I only knew how to begin."
For, you see,
so many out-of-the-way things
had happened lately,
that Alice had begun to think
that very few things indeed
were really impossible.

There seemed to be no use
in waiting by the little door,
so she went back to the table,
half hoping she might find

another key on it,
or at any rate a book of rules
for shutting people up
like telescopes:
this time she found
a little bottle on it,

("which certainly was not here
before, " said Alice,)
and round the neck of the bottle
was a paper label,
with the words "DRINK ME,"
beautifully printed on it
in large letters.

It was all very well to say
"Drink me,"
but the wise little Alice
was not going to do that
in a hurry. "No, I'll look first,"
she said,
"and see whether it's marked
' poison ' or not";
for she had read
several nice little histories
about children
who had got burnt,
and eaten up by wild beasts
and other unpleasant things,
all because they would not
remember the simple rules
their friends had taught them:
such as, that a red-hot poker
will burn you
if you hold it too long;
and that if you cut your finger
very deeply with a knife,
it usually bleeds;
and she had never forgotten that,
if you drink much from a bottle
marked "poison,"
it is almost certain
to disagree with you,
sooner or later.

However, this bottle
was not marked "poison,"
so Alice ventured to taste it,
and finding it very nice,

(it had, in fact, a sort
of mixed flavour of cherry-tart,
custard, pine-apple, roast turkey,
toffee, and hot buttered toast,)
she very soon finished it off.

"What a curious feeling!"
said Alice;
"I must be shutting up
like a telescope."

And so it was indeed:
she was now
only ten inches high,
and her face brightened up
at the thought that she
was now the right size
for going through the little door
into that lovely garden.
First, however,
she waited for a few minutes
to see if she was going
to shrink any further:
she felt a little nervous about this;
"for it might end, you know,"
said Alice to herself,
"in my going out altogether,
like a candle.
I wonder what I
should be like then?"
And she tried to fancy
what the flame of a candle
is like after the candle
is blown out,
for she could not remember
ever having seen such a thing.

After a while, finding that

nothing more happened,
she decided on going
into the garden at once; but,
alas for poor Alice!
when she got to the door,
she found she had forgotten
the little golden key,
and when she went back
to the table for it, she found
she could not possibly reach it:
she could see it quite plainly
through the glass,
and she tried her best to climb up
one of the legs of the table,
but it was too slippery;
and when she had
tired herself out with trying,
the poor little thing
sat down and cried.

"Come,
there's no use in crying like that!"
said Alice to herself,
rather sharply;
"I advise you to leave off
this minute!"
She generally gave herself
very good advice,

(though she very seldom
followed it),
and sometimes
she scolded herself so severely
as to bring tears into her eyes;
and once she remembered trying
to box her own ears
for having cheated herself
in a game of croquet
she was playing against herself,
for this curious child
was very fond of pretending
to be two people.
"But it's no use now,"
thought poor Alice,

"to pretend to be two people!
Why,
there's hardly enough of me left
to make one respectable person!"

Soon her eye fell
on a little glass box
that was lying under the table:
she opened it,
and found in it a very small cake,
on which the words "EAT ME"
were beautifully
marked in currants.
"Well, I'll eat it," said Alice,
"and if it makes me grow larger,
I can reach the key;
and if it makes me grow smaller,
I can creep under the door;
so either way
I'll get into the garden,
and I don't care which happens!"

She ate a little bit,
and said anxiously to herself,
"Which way? Which way?",
holding her hand on the top
of her head to feel
which way it was growing,
and she was quite surprised
to find that she remained
the same size: to be sure,
this generally happens
when one eats cake, but Alice
had got so much into the way
of expecting nothing
but out-of-the-way things
to happen,
that it seemed quite dull
and stupid for life to go on
in the common way.

So she set to work, and very soon
finished off the cake.

CHAPTER II.

The Pool of Tears

"Curiouser and curiouser!"
cried Alice
(she was so much surprised,
that for the moment
she quite forgot
how to speak good English);
"now I'm opening out like the
largest telescope that ever was!
Good-bye, feet!"
(for when she looked down
at her feet,
they seemed to be
almost out of sight,
they were getting so far off).
"Oh, my poor little feet,
I wonder who will put on
your shoes and stockings
for you now, dears?
I'm sure I shan't be able!
I shall be a great deal too far off
to trouble myself about you:
you must manage
the best way you can;
—but I must be kind to them,"
thought Alice,
"or perhaps they won't walk
the way I want to go!
Let me see:
I'll give them a new pair of boots
every Christmas."

And she went on
planning to herself
how she would manage it.
"They must go by the carrier,"
she thought;
"and how funny it'll seem,
sending presents
to one's own feet!
And how odd the directions

will look!
Alice's Right Foot, Esq.,
Hearthrug, near the Fender,

(with Alice's love).

Oh dear,
what nonsense I'm talking!"

Just then her head
struck against the roof of the hall:
in fact she was now
more than nine feet high,
and she at once
took up the little golden key and
hurried off to the garden door.

Poor Alice!
It was as much as she could do,
lying down on one side,
to look through into the garden
with one eye;
but to get through
was more hopeless than ever:
she sat down
and began to cry again.

"You ought to be ashamed
of yourself," said Alice,
"a great girl like you,"
(she might well say this),
"to go on crying in this way!
Stop this moment, I tell you!"
But she went on all the same,
shedding gallons of tears,
until there was a large pool
all round her,
about four inches deep
and reaching half down the hall.

After a time she heard
a little pattering of feet
in the distance,
and she hastily dried her eyes

to see what was coming.
It was the White Rabbit returning,
splendidly dressed,
with a pair of white kid gloves
in one hand and a large fan
in the other:
he came trotting along
in a great hurry,
muttering to himself as he came,
"Oh! the Duchess, the Duchess!
Oh! won't she be savage
if I've kept her waiting!"
Alice felt so desperate
that she was ready
to ask help of any one; so,
when the Rabbit came near her,
she began, in a low, timid voice,
"If you please,sir—"
The Rabbit started violently,
dropped the white kid gloves
and the fan,
and skurried away
into the darkness
as hard as he could go.

Alice took up the fan and gloves,
and, as the hall was very hot,
she kept fanning herself
all the time she went on talking:
"Dear, dear!
How queer everything is to-day!
And yesterday
things went on just as usual.
I wonder if I've been changed
in the night? Let me think:
was I the same
when I got up this morning?
I almost think I can remember
feeling a little different.
But if I'm not the same,
the next question is,
Who in the world am I? Ah,
that's the great puzzle!"
And she began thinking

over all the children she knew
that were of the same age
as herself,
to see if she could have been
changed for any of them.

"I'm sure I'm not Ada," she said,
"for her hair goes
in such long ringlets,
and mine doesn't go
in ringlets at all;
and I'm sure I can't be Mabel,
for I know all sorts of things,
and she, oh!
she knows such a very little!
Besides, she's she, and I'm I,
and—oh dear,
how puzzling it all is!
I'll try if I know all the things
I used to know. Let me see:
four times five is twelve,
and four times six is thirteen,
and four times seven is—oh dear!
I shall never get to twenty
at that rate! However,
the Multiplication Table
doesn't signify:
let's try Geography.
London is the capital of Paris,
and Paris is the capital of Rome,
and Rome—no, that's all wrong,
I'm certain!
I must have been changed
for Mabel!
I'll try and say
' How doth the little —' " and
she crossed her hands on her lap
as if she were saying lessons,
and began to repeat it,
but her voice sounded hoarse
and strange,
and the words did not come
the same as they used to do:—

"How doth the little crocodile
    Improve his shining tail,

And pour the waters of the Nile
    On every golden scale!

"How cheerfully
                he seems to grin,
    How neatly spread his claws,
And welcome little fishes in
    With gently smiling jaws!"

"I'm sure those are not
the right words," said poor Alice,
and her eyes filled
with tears again as she went on,
"I must be Mabel after all,
and I shall have to go and live
in that poky little house,
and have next to no toys
to play with, and oh!
ever so many lessons to learn!
No,
I've made up my mind about it;
if I'm Mabel, I'll stay down here!
It'll be no use their putting
their heads down and saying
 'Come up again, dear!'
I shall only look up and say
 'Who am I then?
Tell me that first, and then,
if I like being that person,
I'll come up: if not,
I'll stay down here till
I'm somebody else'—but,
oh dear!" cried Alice,
with a sudden burst of tears,
"I do wish they would put
their heads down!
I am so very tired
of being all alone here!"

As she said this she looked down
at her hands,
and was surprised to see
that she had put on one
of the Rabbit's
little white kid gloves
while she was talking.
"How can I have done that?"
she thought.
"I must be growing small again."
She got up and went to the table
to measure herself by it,
and found that,
as nearly as she could guess,
she was now about two feet high,
and was going on
shrinking rapidly:
she soon found out
that the cause of this
was the fan she was holding,
and she dropped it hastily,
just in time to avoid
shrinking away altogether.

"That was a narrow escape!"
said Alice,
a good deal frightened
at the sudden change,
but very glad to find herself
still in existence;
"and now for the garden!"
and she ran with all speed
back to the little door: but, alas!
the little door was shut again,
and the little golden key
was lying on the glass table
as before,
"and things are worse than ever,"
thought the poor child,
"for I never was so small
as this before, never!
And I declare it's too bad,
that it is!"

As she said these words
her foot slipped,

and in another moment,
splash!
she was up to her chin
in salt water.
Her first idea
was that she had somehow
fallen into the sea,
"and in that case I can go back
by railway," she said to herself.

(Alice had been to the seaside
once in her life, and had come
to the general conclusion,
that wherever you go to
on the English coast
you find a number
of bathing machines in the sea,
some children digging
in the sand with wooden spades,
then a row of lodging houses,
and behind them
a railway station.) However,
she soon made out that
she was in the pool of tears
which she had wept
when she was nine feet high.

"I wish I hadn't cried so much!"
said Alice, as she swam about,
trying to find her way out.
"I shall be punished for it now,
I suppose, by being drowned
in my own tears!
That will be a queer thing,
to be sure! However,
everything is queer to-day."

Just then she heard
something splashing
about in the pool a little way off,
and she swam nearer
to make out what it was:
at first she thought
it must be a walrus

or hippopotamus,
but then she remembered
how small she was now,
and she soon made out
that it was only a mouse
that had slipped in like herself.

"Would it be of any use, now,"
thought Alice,
"to speak to this mouse?
Everything is so
out-of-the-way down here,
that I should think very likely
it can talk: at any rate,
there's no harm in trying.
" So she began: "O Mouse,
do you know the way out
of this pool?
I am very tired
of swimming about here,
O Mouse!"
(Alice thought this must be
the right way
of speaking to a mouse:
she had never done
such a thing before,
but she remembered
having seen
in her brother's Latin Grammar,
"A mouse—of a mouse—to a
mouse—a mouse—O mouse!")
The Mouse looked at her
rather inquisitively,
and seemed to her to wink
with one of its little eyes,
but it said nothing.

"Perhaps
it doesn't understand English,"
thought Alice;
"I daresay it's a French mouse,
come over
with William the Conqueror."
(For,

with all her knowledge of history,
Alice had no very clear notion
how long ago
anything had happened.)
So she began again:
"Où est ma chatte?"
which was the first sentence
in her French lesson-book.
The Mouse gave a sudden leap
out of the water,
and seemed to quiver all over
with fright.
"Oh, I beg your pardon!"
cried Alice hastily,
afraid that she had hurt
the poor animal's feelings.
"I quite forgot
you didn't like cats."

"Not like cats!" cried the Mouse,
in a shrill, passionate voice.
"Would you like cats
if you were me?"

"Well, perhaps not,"
said Alice in a soothing tone:
"don't be angry about it.
And yet I wish I could show you
our cat Dinah:
I think you'd take a fancy
to cats if you could only see her.
She is such a dear quiet thing,
" Alice went on, half to herself,
as she swam lazily about
in the pool,
"and she sits purring
so nicely by the fire,
licking her paws
and washing her face—
and she is such
a nice soft thing to nurse—
and she's such a capital one
for catching mice—oh,
I beg your pardon!"

cried Alice again,
for this time the Mouse
was bristling all over,
and she felt certain
it must be really offended.
"We won't talk about her
any more if you'd rather not."

"We indeed!" cried the Mouse,
who was trembling down
to the end of his tail.
"As if I would talk
on such a subject!
Our family always hated cats:
nasty, low, vulgar things!
Don't let me hear
the name again!"

"I won't indeed!" said Alice,
in a great hurry
to change the subject
of conversation.
"Are you—are you fond—
of—of dogs?"
The Mouse did not answer,
so Alice went on eagerly:
"There is such a nice little dog
near our house
I should like to show you!
A little bright-eyed terrier,
you know, with oh,
such long curly brown hair!
And it'll fetch things
when you throw them,
and it'll sit up
and beg for its dinner,
and all sorts of things—
I can't remember half of them—
and it belongs to a farmer,
you know,
and he says it's so useful,
it's worth a hundred pounds!
He says it kills
all the rats and—oh dear!"

cried Alice in a sorrowful tone,
"I'm afraid
I've offended it again!"
For the Mouse was swimming
away from her
as hard as it could go,
and making quite a commotion
in the pool as it went.

So she called softly after it,
"Mouse dear!
Do come back again,
and we won't talk about cats
or dogs either,
if you don't like them!"
When the Mouse heard this,
it turned round and swam slowly
back to her:
its face was quite pale
(with passion, Alice thought),
and it said in a low trembling
voice, "Let us get to the shore,
and then I'll tell you my history,
and you'll understand
why it is I hate cats and dogs."

It was high time to go,
for the pool
was getting quite crowded
with the birds and animals
that had fallen into it:
there were a Duck and a Dodo,
a Lory and an Eaglet, and several
other curious creatures.
Alice led the way,
and the whole party
swam to the shore.

CHAPTER III.

A Caucus-Race
and a Long Tale

They were indeed
a queer-looking party
that assembled on the bank—
the birds with draggled feathers,
the animals with their fur
clinging close to them,
and all dripping wet, cross,
and uncomfortable.

The first question of course was,
how to get dry again:
they had a consultation
about this,
and after a few minutes
it seemed quite natural
to Alice to find herself
talking familiarly with them,
as if she had known them
all her life. Indeed,
she had quite a long argument
with the Lory,
who at last turned sulky,
and would only say,
"I am older than you,
and must know better;"
and this Alice would not allow
without knowing how old it was,
and,
as the Lory positively refused
to tell its age,
there was no more to be said.

At last the Mouse,
who seemed to be a person
of authority among them,
called out, "Sit down,
all of you, and listen to me!
I'll soon make you dry enough!"
They all sat down at once,

in a large ring,
with the Mouse in the middle.
Alice kept her eyes
anxiously fixed on it,
for she felt sure she would
catch a bad cold
if she did not get dry very soon.

"Ahem!" said the Mouse
with an important air,
"are you all ready?
This is the driest thing I know.
Silence all round, if you please!
'William the Conqueror,
whose cause
was favoured by the pope,
was soon submitted to
by the English,
who wanted leaders,
and had been of late
much accustomed
to usurpation and conquest.
Edwin and Morcar,
the earls of Mercia
and Northumbria—' "

"Ugh!" said the Lory,
with a shiver.

"I beg your pardon!"
said the Mouse, frowning,
but very politely:
"Did you speak?"

"Not I!" said the Lory hastily.

"I thought you did,"
said the Mouse."—I proceed.
'Edwin and Morcar,
the earls of Mercia
and Northumbria,
declared for him:
and even Stigand,
the patriotic archbishop

of Canterbury,
found it advisable—' "

"Found what ?" said the Duck.

"Found it ," the Mouse replied
rather crossly:
"of course you know
what 'it' means."

"I know what 'it'
means well enough,
when I find a thing,"
said the Duck:
"it's generally a frog or a worm.
The question is,
what did the archbishop find?"

The Mouse did not notice
this question,
but hurriedly went on,
" '—found it advisable to go
with Edgar Atheling
to meet William
and offer him the crown.
William's conduct
at first was moderate.
But the insolence
of his Normans—'
How are you getting on now,
my dear?" it continued,
turning to Alice as it spoke.

"As wet as ever,"
said Alice in a melancholy tone:
"it doesn't seem to dry me at all."

"In that case,"
said the Dodo solemnly,
rising to its feet,
"I move that the meeting adjourn,
for the immediate adoption
of more energetic remedies—"

"Speak English!" said the Eaglet.
"I don't know the meaning
of half those long words,
and, what's more,
I don't believe you do either!"
And the Eaglet bent down
its head to hide a smile:
some of the other birds
tittered audibly.

"What I was going to say,"
said the Dodo
in an offended tone, "was,
that the best thing to get us dry
would be a Caucus-race."

"What is a Caucus-race?"
said Alice;
not that she wanted
much to know,
but the Dodo had paused
as if it thought
that somebody ought to speak,
and no one else
seemed inclined to say anything.

"Why," said the Dodo,
"the best way
to explain it is to do it."
(And, as you might like to try
the thing yourself,
some winter day,
I will tell you how
the Dodo managed it.)

First it marked out a race-course,
in a sort of circle,

("the exact shape doesn't matter,"
it said,) and then all the party
were placed along the course,
here and there.
There was no "One, two,
three, and away,"

but they began running
when they liked,
and left off when they liked,
so that it was not easy to know
when the race was over.
However,
when they had been running
half an hour or so,
and were quite dry again,
the Dodo suddenly called out
"The race is over!"
and they all crowded round it,
panting, and asking,
"But who has won?"

This question the Dodo
could not answer
without a great deal of thought,
and it sat for a long time
with one finger
pressed upon its forehead
(the position in which you
usually see Shakespeare,
in the pictures of him),
while the rest waited in silence.
At last the Dodo said,
"Everybody has won,
and all must have prizes."

"But who is to give the prizes?"
quite a chorus of voices asked.

"Why, she , of course,"
said the Dodo,
pointing to Alice with one finger;
and the whole party
at once crowded round her,
calling out in a confused way,
"Prizes! Prizes!"

Alice had no idea what to do,
and in despair
she put her hand in her pocket,
and pulled out a box of comfits,
(luckily the salt water
had not got into it),
and handed them round
as prizes.
There was exactly one a-piece,
all round.

"But she must have
a prize herself, you know,"
said the Mouse.

"Of course,"
the Dodo replied very gravely.
"What else have you got
in your pocket?" he went on,
turning to Alice.

"Only a thimble,"
said Alice sadly.

"Hand it over here,"
said the Dodo.

Then they all crowded
round her once more,
while the Dodo solemnly
presented the thimble,
saying "We beg your acceptance
of this elegant thimble;" and,
when it had finished
this short speech,
they all cheered.

Alice thought
the whole thing very absurd,
but they all looked so grave
that she did not dare to laugh;
and,
as she could not think
of anything to say,
she simply bowed,
and took the thimble,
looking as solemn as she could.

The next thing was
to eat the comfits:
this caused some noise
and confusion,
as the large birds complained
that they could not taste theirs,
and the small ones choked
and had to be patted on the back.
However, it was over at last,
and they sat down again
in a ring,
and begged the Mouse
to tell them something more.

"You promised to tell me
your history, you know,"
said Alice,
"and why it is you hate—
C and D,"
she added in a whisper,
half afraid that it would be
offended again.

"Mine is a long and a sad tale!"
said the Mouse,
turning to Alice, and sighing.

"It is a long tail, certainly,"
said Alice,
looking down with wonder
at the Mouse's tail;
"but why do you call it sad?"
And she kept on puzzling
about it while
the Mouse was speaking,
so that her idea of the tale
was something like this:—

"Fury said to a mouse,
That he met in the house,
'Let us both go to law:
I will prosecute you. —Come,
I'll take no denial;

We must have a trial:
For really this morning
I've nothing to do.'
Said the mouse to the cur,
 'Such a trial, dear sir,
With no jury or judge,
would be wasting our breath.'
 'I'll be judge, I'll be jury,'
Said cunning old Fury:
 'I'll try the whole cause,
and condemn you to death.' "

"You are not attending!"
said the Mouse to Alice severely.
"What are you thinking of?"

"I beg your pardon,"
said Alice very humbly:
"you had got to the fifth bend,
I think?"

"I had not!" cried the Mouse,
sharply and very angrily.

"A knot!" said Alice,
always ready
to make herself useful,
and looking anxiously about her.
"Oh, do let me help to undo it!"

"I shall do nothing of the sort,"
said the Mouse,
getting up and walking away.
"You insult me
by talking such nonsense!"

"I didn't mean it!"
pleaded poor Alice.
"But you're so easily offended,
you know!"

The Mouse only growled in reply.

"Please come back

and finish your story!"
Alice called after it;
and the others
all joined in chorus,
"Yes, please do!" but the Mouse
only shook its head impatiently,
and walked a little quicker.

"What a pity it wouldn't stay!"
sighed the Lory, as soon as it was
quite out of sight;
and an old Crab
took the opportunity
of saying to her daughter
"Ah, my dear!
Let this be a lesson to you
never to lose your temper!"
"Hold your tongue, Ma!"
said the young Crab,
a little snappishly.
"You're enough
to try the patience of an oyster!"

"I wish I had our Dinah here,
I know I do!" said Alice aloud,
addressing nobody in particular.
"She'd soon fetch it back!"

"And who is Dinah,
if I might venture
to ask the question?"
said the Lory.

Alice replied eagerly,
for she was always ready
to talk about her pet:
"Dinah's our cat.
And she's such a capital one
for catching mice you can't think!
And oh,
I wish you could see her
after the birds! Why,
she'll eat a little bird
as soon as look at it!"

This speech caused a remarkable
sensation among the party.
Some of the birds
hurried off at once:
one old Magpie
began wrapping itself up
very carefully, remarking,
"I really must be getting home;
the night-air doesn't suit
my throat!"
and a Canary called out
in a trembling voice
to its children,
"Come away, my dears!
It's high time
you were all in bed!"
On various pretexts
they all moved off,
and Alice was soon left alone.

"I wish I hadn't
mentioned Dinah!"
she said to herself
in a melancholy tone.
"Nobody seems to like her,
down here, and I'm sure
she's the best cat in the world!
Oh, my dear Dinah!
I wonder if I shall ever
see you any more!"
And here poor Alice
began to cry again,
for she felt very lonely
and low-spirited.
In a little while, however,
she again heard a little pattering
of footsteps in the distance,
and she looked up eagerly,
half hoping that the Mouse
had changed his mind,
and was coming back
to finish his story.

CHAPTER IV.

The Rabbit Sends in
a Little Bill

It was the White Rabbit,
trotting slowly back again,
and looking anxiously about
as it went,
as if it had lost something;
and she heard it muttering to
itself "The Duchess!
The Duchess!
Oh my dear paws!
Oh my fur and whiskers!
She'll get me executed,
as sure as ferrets are ferrets!
Where can I have dropped them,
I wonder?"
Alice guessed in a moment
that it was looking for the fan
and the pair of white kid gloves,
and she very good-naturedly
began hunting about for them,
but they were nowhere
to be seen—
everything seemed
to have changed
since her swim in the pool,
and the great hall,
with the glass table
and the little door,
had vanished completely.

Very soon the Rabbit
noticed Alice,
as she went hunting about,
and called out to her
in an angry tone,
"Why, Mary Ann,
what are you doing out here?
Run home this moment,
and fetch me a pair of gloves
and a fan! Quick, now!"

And Alice
was so much frightened
that she ran off at once
in the direction it pointed to,
without trying to explain
the mistake it had made.

"He took me for his housemaid,"
she said to herself as she ran.
"How surprised he'll be
when he finds out who I am!
But I'd better take him his fan
and gloves—that is,
if I can find them."
As she said this,
she came upon a neat little house,
on the door of which
was a bright brass plate
with the name "W. RABBIT,"
engraved upon it.
She went in without knocking,
and hurried upstairs,
in great fear lest she should meet
the real Mary Ann,
and be turned out of the house
before she had found the fan
and gloves.

"How queer it seems,"
Alice said to herself,
"to be going messages
for a rabbit!
I suppose Dinah'll be sending me
on messages next!"
And she began fancying the sort
of thing that would happen:
"'Miss Alice! Come here directly,
and get ready for your walk!'
'Coming in a minute, nurse!
But I've got to see that
the mouse doesn't get out.'
Only I don't think,"
Alice went on,
"that they'd let Dinah stop

in the house if it began
ordering people about like that!"
By this time she had
found her way into
a tidy little room
with a table in the window,
and on it
(as she had hoped) a fan
and two or three pairs
of tiny white kid gloves:
she took up the fan
and a pair of the gloves,
and was just going
to leave the room,
when her eye fell upon
a little bottle that stood
near the looking-glass.
There was no label this time
with the words "DRINK ME,"
but nevertheless she uncorked it
and put it to her lips.
"I know something interesting
is sure to happen,"
she said to herself,
"whenever I eat
or drink anything;
so I'll just see
what this bottle does.
I do hope it'll make me
grow large again,
for really I'm quite tired
of being such a tiny little thing!"

It did so indeed,
and much sooner
than she had expected:
before she had drunk
half the bottle,
she found her head
pressing against the ceiling,
and had to stoop to save her neck
from being broken.
She hastily put down the bottle,
saying to herself

"That's quite enough—
I hope I shan't grow any more—
As it is,
I can't get out at the door—
I do wish I hadn't drunk
quite so much!"

Alas!
it was too late to wish that!
She went on growing,
and growing,
and very soon had to kneel down
on the floor:
in another minute
there was not even room for this,
and she tried the effect
of lying down with one elbow
against the door,
and the other arm
curled round her head.
Still she went on growing,
and, as a last resource,
she put one arm
out of the window,
and one foot up the chimney,
and said to herself
"Now I can do no more,
whatever happens.
What will become of me?"

Luckily for Alice,
the little magic bottle
had now had its full effect,
and she grew no larger:
still it was very uncomfortable,
and,
as there seemed to be no sort
of chance of her ever getting out
of the room again,
no wonder she felt unhappy.

"It was much pleasanter
at home," thought poor Alice,
"when one wasn't always

growing larger and smaller,
and being ordered about
by mice and rabbits.
I almost wish I hadn't gone down
that rabbit-hole—and yet—
and yet—it's rather curious,
you know, this sort of life!
I do wonder what can have
happened to me!
When I used to read fairy-tales,
I fancied that kind of thing
never happened,
and now here I am
in the middle of one!
There ought to be a book
written about me,
that there ought!
And when I grow up,
I'll write one—
but I'm grown up now,"
she added in a sorrowful tone;
"at least there's no room
to grow up any more here ."

"But then," thought Alice,
"shall I never get any older
than I am now?
That'll be a comfort, one way—
never to be an old woman—
but then—
always to have lessons to learn!
Oh, I shouldn't like that!"

"Oh, you foolish Alice!"
she answered herself.
"How can you learn lessons
in here? Why,
there's hardly room for you ,
and no room at all
for any lesson-books!"

And so she went on,
taking first one side
and then the other,

and making quite a conversation
of it altogether;
but after a few minutes
she heard a voice outside,
and stopped to listen.

"Mary Ann! Mary Ann!"
said the voice.
"Fetch me my gloves
this moment!"
Then came a little pattering of feet
on the stairs.
Alice knew it was the Rabbit
coming to look for her,
and she trembled
till she shook the house,
quite forgetting that she was now
about a thousand times
as large as the Rabbit,
and had no reason
to be afraid of it.

Presently the Rabbit
came up to the door,
and tried to open it; but,
as the door opened inwards,
and Alice's elbow
was pressed hard against it,
that attempt proved a failure.
Alice heard it say to itself
"Then I'll go round
and get in at the window."

"That you won't!" thought Alice,
and, after waiting till she fancied
she heard the Rabbit
just under the window,
she suddenly
spread out her hand,
and made a snatch in the air.
She did not get hold of anything,
but she heard
a little shriek and a fall,
and a crash of broken glass,

from which she concluded
that it was just possible
it had fallen
into a cucumber-frame,
or something of the sort.

Next came an angry voice—
the Rabbit's—"Pat! Pat!
Where are you?"
And then a voice
she had never heard before,
"Sure then I'm here!
Digging for apples,
yer honour!"

"Digging for apples, indeed!"
said the Rabbit angrily. "Here!
Come and help me out of this! "
(Sounds of more broken glass.)

"Now tell me, Pat,
what's that in the window?"

"Sure, it's an arm, yer honour!"
(He pronounced it "arrum.")

"An arm, you goose!
Who ever saw one that size?
Why, it fills the whole window!"

"Sure, it does, yer honour:
but it's an arm for all that."

"Well, it's got no business there,
at any rate: go and take it away!"

There was a long silence
after this, and Alice
could only hear whispers
now and then; such as,
"Sure, I don't like it,
yer honour, at all, at all!"
"Do as I tell you, you coward!"
and at last she spread out

her hand again,
and made another snatch
in the air. This time
there were two little shrieks,
and more sounds of broken glass.
"What a number
of cucumber-frames
there must be!" thought Alice.
"I wonder what they'll do next!
As for pulling me
out of the window,
I only wish they could!
I'm sure I don't want
to stay in here any longer!"

She waited for some time
without hearing anything more:
at last came a rumbling
of little cartwheels,
and the sound
of a good many voices
all talking together:
she made out the words:
"Where's the other ladder?—
Why, I hadn't to bring but one;
Bill's got the other—Bill!
fetch it here, lad! —Here,
put 'em up at this corner—No,
tie 'em together first—
they don't reach
half high enough yet—Oh!
they'll do well enough;
don't be particular—Here, Bill!
catch hold of this rope—
Will the roof bear? —
Mind that loose slate—Oh,
it's coming down! Heads below!"
(a loud crash)—"Now,
who did that? —It was Bill,
I fancy—Who's to go down the
chimney?
—Nay, I shan't! You do it!
— That I won't, then!
—Bill's to go down—Here, Bill!

the master says you're to go
down the chimney!"

"Oh! So Bill's got to come down
the chimney, has he?"
said Alice to herself. "Shy,
they seem to put everything
upon Bill!
I wouldn't be in Bill's place
for a good deal:
this fireplace is narrow,
to be sure;
but I think I can kick a little!
"

She drew her foot as far down
the chimney as she could,
and waited till she heard
a little animal
(she couldn't guess
of what sort it was)
scratching and scrambling
about in the chimney
close above her: then,
saying to herself "This is Bill,"
she gave one sharp kick,
and waited to see
what would happen next.

The first thing she heard
was a general chorus
of "There goes Bill!"
then the Rabbit's voice along—
"Catch him, you by the hedge!"
then silence,
and then another confusion
of voices—"Hold up his head—
Brandy now—
Don't choke him—
How was it, old fellow?
What happened to you?
Tell us all about it!"

Last came a little feeble,

squeaking voice,

("That's Bill," thought Alice,)
"Well, I hardly know—No more,
thank ye; I'm better now—
but I'm a deal too flustered
to tell you—all I know is,
something comes at me
like a Jack-in-the-box,
and up I goes like a sky-rocket!"

"So you did, old fellow!"
said the others.

"We must burn the house down!"
said the Rabbit's voice;
and Alice called out
as loud as she could,
"If you do, I'll set Dinah at you!"

There was a dead silence
instantly,
and Alice thought to herself,
"I wonder what they will do next!
If they had any sense,
they'd take the roof off."
After a minute or two,
they began moving about again,
and Alice heard the Rabbit say,
"A barrowful will do,
to begin with."

"A barrowful of what?"
thought Alice;
but she had not long to doubt,
for the next moment a shower
of little pebbles
came rattling in at the window,
and some of them hit her
in the face.
"I'll put a stop to this,"
she said to herself,
and shouted out,
"You'd better not do that again!"

which produced
another dead silence.

Alice noticed with some surprise
that the pebbles
were all turning into little cakes
as they lay on the floor,
and a bright idea
came into her head.
"If I eat one of these cakes,"
she thought,
"it's sure to make some change
in my size; and as it can't
possibly make me larger,
it must make me smaller,
I suppose."

So she swallowed
one of the cakes,
and was delighted to find
that she began shrinking directly.
As soon as she was small enough
to get through the door,
she ran out of the house,
and found quite a crowd
of little animals and birds
waiting outside.
The poor little Lizard, Bill,
was in the middle,
being held up
by two guinea-pigs,
who were giving it
something out of a bottle.
They all made a rush at Alice
the moment she appeared;
but she ran off as hard
as she could,
and soon found herself
safe in a thick wood.

"The first thing I've got to do,"
said Alice to herself,
as she wandered about
in the wood,

"is to grow to my right size again;
and the second thing is to find
my way into that lovely garden.
I think that will be the best plan."

It sounded an excellent plan,
no doubt, and very neatly
and simply arranged;
the only difficulty was,
that she had not the smallest idea
how to set about it;
and while she was peering about
anxiously among the trees,
a little sharp bark
just over her head
made her look up
in a great hurry.

An enormous puppy
was looking down at her
with large round eyes,
and feebly stretching out
one paw, trying to touch her.
"Poor little thing! " said Alice,
in a coaxing tone,
and she tried hard to whistle to it;
but she was terribly frightened
all the time at the thought
that it might be hungry,
in which case it would be
very likely to eat her up
in spite of all her coaxing.

Hardly knowing what she did,
she picked up a little bit of stick,
and held it out to the puppy;
whereupon the puppy
jumped into the air
off all its feet at once,
with a yelp of delight,
and rushed at the stick,
and made believe to worry it;
then Alice dodged
behind a great thistle,

to keep herself
from being run over;
and the moment
she appeared on the other side,
the puppy made another rush
at the stick,
and tumbled head over heels
in its hurry to get hold of it;
then Alice,
thinking it was very like having
a game of play with a cart-horse,
and expecting every moment
to be trampled under its feet,
ran round the thistle again;
then the puppy began a series
of short charges at the stick,
running
a very little way forwards
each time and a long way back,
and barking hoarsely
all the while,
till at last it sat down
a good way off, panting,
with its tongue hanging
out of its mouth,
and its great eyes half shut.

This seemed to Alice
a good opportunity
for making her escape;
so she set off at once,
and ran till she was quite tired
and out of breath,
and till the puppy's bark
sounded quite faint
in the distance.

"And yet what a dear little puppy
it was!" said Alice,
as she leant against a buttercup
to rest herself,
and fanned herself
with one of the leaves:
"I should have liked

teaching it tricks very much,
if—if I'd only been
the right size to do it! Oh dear!
I'd nearly forgotten
that I've got to grow up again!
Let me see—
how is it to be managed?
I suppose I ought to eat or drink
something or other;
but the great question is, what?"

The great question certainly was,
what?
Alice looked all round her
at the flowers
and the blades of grass,
but she did not see anything
that looked like
the right thing to eat or drink
under the circumstances.
There was a large mushroom
growing near her,
about the same height as herself;
and when she had
looked under it,
and on both sides of it,
and behind it,
it occurred to her
that she might as well look
and see what was on the top of it.

She stretched herself up on tiptoe,
and peeped over the edge
of the mushroom,
and her eyes
immediately met those
of a large blue caterpillar,
that was sitting on the top
with its arms folded,
quietly smoking a long hookah,
and taking not
the smallest notice of her
or of anything else.

CHAPTER V.

Advice from a Caterpillar

The Caterpillar and Alice
looked at each other
for some time in silence:
at last the Caterpillar
took the hookah out of its mouth,
and addressed her in a languid,
sleepy voice.

"Who are you?"
said the Caterpillar.

This was not an encouraging
opening for a conversation.
Alice replied, rather shyly,
"I—I hardly know, sir,
just at present—
at least I know who I was
when I got up this morning,
but I think
I must have been changed
several times since then."

"What do you mean by that?"
said the Caterpillar sternly.
"Explain yourself!"

"I can't explain myself,
I'm afraid, sir," said Alice,
"because I'm not myself,
you see."

"I don't see," said the Caterpillar.

"I'm afraid
I can't put it more clearly,"
Alice replied very politely,
"for I can't understand it myself
to begin with;
and being so many different sizes
in a day is very confusing."

"It isn't," said the Caterpillar.

"Well, perhaps you
haven't found it so yet,"
said Alice;
"but when you have to turn into
a chrysalis—you will some day,
you know—and then after that
into a butterfly,
I should think you'll feel it
a little queer, won't you?"

"Not a bit," said the Caterpillar.

"Well, perhaps your feelings
may be different," said Alice;
"all I know is,
it would feel very queer to me .
"

"You!" said the Caterpillar
contemptuously.
"Who are you?"

Which brought them
back again to the beginning
of the conversation.
Alice felt a little irritated
at the Caterpillar's
making such very short remarks,
and she drew herself up and said,
very gravely, "I think,
you ought to tell me who you are,
first."

"Why?" said the Caterpillar.

Here was another
puzzling question;
and as Alice could not think of
any good reason,
and as the Caterpillar seemed
to be in a very unpleasant state

of mind, she turned away.

"Come back!"
the Caterpillar called after her.
"I've something important
to say!"

This sounded promising,
certainly: Alice turned
and came back again.

"Keep your temper,"
said the Caterpillar.

"Is that all?" said Alice,
swallowing down her anger
as well as she could.

"No," said the Caterpillar.

Alice thought
she might as well wait,
as she had nothing else to do,
and perhaps after all it might
tell her something worth hearing.
For some minutes it puffed away
without speaking,
but at last it unfolded its arms,
took the hookah
out of its mouth again, and said,
"So you think you're changed,
do you?"

"I'm afraid I am, sir," said Alice;
"I can't remember things
as I used—
and I don't keep the same size
for ten minutes together!"

"Can't remember what things?"
said the Caterpillar.

"Well, I've tried to say
"How doth the little busy bee,"

but it all came different!"
Alice replied
in a very melancholy voice.

"Repeat,"
You are old, Father William,' "
said the Caterpillar.

Alice folded her hands,
and began:—

"You are old, Father William,"
the young man said,
    "And your hair
      has become very white;
And yet you incessantly
stand on your head—
    Do you think,
      at your age, it is right?"

"In my youth," Father William
replied to his son,
    "I feared it might
      injure the brain;
But,
now that I'm perfectly sure
I have none,
    Why, I do it again and again."

"You are old," said the youth,"
as I mentioned before,
    And have grown
      most uncommonly fat;
Yet you turned a back-somersault
in at the door—
    Pray,
      what is the reason of that?"

"In my youth," said the sage,
as he shook his grey locks,
    "I kept all my limbs
      very supple
By the use of this ointment—
one shilling the box—

Allow me to sell you a couple?"

"You are old," said the youth,
"and your jaws are too weak
    For anything tougher
    than suet;
Yet you finished the goose,
with the bones and the beak—
    Pray, how did you
    manage to do it?"

"In my youth," said his father,
"I took to the law,
    And argued each case
    with my wife;
And the muscular strength,
which it gave to my jaw,
    Has lasted
    the rest of my life."

"You are old," said the youth,
"one would hardly suppose
    That your eye
    was as steady as ever;
Yet you balanced an eel
on the end of your nose—
    What made you
    so awfully clever?"

"I have answered three questions,
and that is enough,"
    Said his father;
    "don't give yourself airs!
Do you think I can listen all day
to such stuff?
    Be off,
    or I'll kick you down stairs!"

"That is not said right,"
said the Caterpillar.

"Not quite right, I'm afraid,"
said Alice, timidly;
"some of the words

have got altered."

"It is wrong
from beginning to end,"
said the Caterpillar decidedly,
and there was silence
for some minutes.

The Caterpillar
was the first to speak.

"What size do you want to be?"
it asked.

"Oh,
I'm not particular as to size,"
Alice hastily replied;
"only one doesn't like
changing so often, you know."

"I don't know,"
said the Caterpillar.

Alice said nothing:
she had never been
so much contradicted
in her life before,
and she felt that she
was losing her temper.

"Are you content now?"
said the Caterpillar.

"Well,
I should like to be a little larger,
sir, if you wouldn't mind,"
said Alice:
"three inches is such
a wretched height to be."

"It is a very good height indeed!"
said the Caterpillar angrily,
rearing itself upright as it spoke
(it was exactly three inches high).

"But I'm not used to it!"
pleaded poor Alice
in a piteous tone.
And she thought of herself,
"I wish the creatures
wouldn't be so easily offended!"

"You'll get used to it in time,"
said the Caterpillar;
and it put the hookah
into its mouth
and began smoking again.

This time Alice waited patiently
until it chose to speak again.
In a minute or two the Caterpillar
took the hookah out of its mouth
and yawned once or twice,
and shook itself.
Then it got down off
the mushroom,
and crawled away in the grass,
merely remarking as it went,
"One side will make you
grow taller,
and the other side
will make you grow shorter."

"One side of what?
The other side of what?"
thought Alice to herself.

"Of the mushroom,"
said the Caterpillar,
just as if she had asked it aloud;
and in another moment
it was out of sight.

Alice remained looking
thoughtfully at the mushroom
for a minute,
trying to make out
which were the two sides of it;

and as it was perfectly round,
she found this
a very difficult question.
However,
at last she stretched her arms
round it as far as they would go,
and broke off a bit of the edge
with each hand.

"And now which is which?"
she said to herself,
and nibbled a little
of the right-hand bit
to try the effect:
the next moment she felt
a violent blow
underneath her chin:
it had struck her foot!

She was a good deal frightened
by this very sudden change,
but she felt that there was
no time to be lost,
as she was shrinking rapidly;
so she set to work at once
to eat some of the other bit.
Her chin was pressed so closely
against her foot,
that there was hardly room
to open her mouth;
but she did it at last,
and managed to swallow
a morsel of the lefthand bit.

"Come, my head's free at last!"
said Alice in a tone of delight,
which changed into alarm
in another moment,
when she found that
her shoulders were nowhere
to be found:
all she could see,
when she looked down,
was an immense length of neck,

which seemed to rise like a stalk
out of a sea of green leaves
that lay far below her.

"What can all
that green stuff be?" said Alice.
"And where have my shoulders
got to? And oh, my poor hands,
how is it I can't see you?"
She was moving them about
as she spoke,
but no result seemed to follow,
except a little shaking among
the distant green leaves.

As there seemed to be no chance
of getting her hands up
to her head,
she tried to get her head down
to them,
and was delighted to find
that her neck would bend
about easily in any direction,
like a serpent.
She had just succeeded
in curving it down
into a graceful zigzag,
and was going to dive in
among the leaves,
which she found to be
nothing but the tops
of the trees under which
she had been wandering,
when a sharp hiss
made her draw back in a hurry:
a large pigeon
had flown into her face,
and was beating her violently
with its wings.

"Serpent!" screamed the Pigeon.

"I'm not a serpent!"
said Alice indignantly.

"Let me alone!"

"Serpent, I say again!"
repeated the Pigeon,
but in a more subdued tone,
and added with a kind of sob,
"I've tried every way,
and nothing seems to suit them!"

"I haven't the least idea
what you're talking about,"
said Alice.

"I've tried the roots of trees,
and I've tried banks,
and I've tried hedges,"
the Pigeon went on,
without attending to her;
"but those serpents!
There's no pleasing them!"

Alice
was more and more puzzled,
but she thought there was no use
in saying anything more
till the Pigeon had finished.

"As if it wasn't trouble enough
hatching the eggs,"
said the Pigeon;
"but I must be on the look-out
for serpents night and day! Why,
I haven't had a wink of sleep
these three weeks!"

"I'm very sorry
you've been annoyed," said Alice,
who was beginning to see
its meaning.

"And just as I'd taken
the highest tree in the wood,"
continued the Pigeon,
raising its voice to a shriek,

"and just as I was thinking
I should be free of them at last,
they must needs come wriggling
down from the sky!
Ugh, Serpent!"

"But I'm not a serpent, I tell you!"
said Alice. "I'm a—I'm a—"

"Well! What are you?"
said the Pigeon.
"I can see you're trying
to invent something!"

"I—I'm a little girl," said Alice,
rather doubtfully,
as she remembered
the number of changes
she had gone through that day.

"A likely story indeed!"
said the Pigeon
in a tone of the deepest contempt.
"I've seen a good many little girls
in my time, but never one
with such a neck as that!
No, no! You're a serpent;
and there's no use denying it.
I suppose
you'll be telling me next
that you never tasted an egg!"

"I have tasted eggs, certainly,"
said Alice,
who was a very truthful child;
"but little girls eat eggs
quite as much as serpents do,
you know."

"I don't believe it,"
said the Pigeon; "but if they do,
why then they're a kind
of serpent, that's all I can say."

This was such a new idea
to Alice,
that she was quite silent
for a minute or two,
which gave the Pigeon
the opportunity of adding,
"You're looking for eggs,
I know that well enough;
and what does it matter to me
whether you're a little girl
or a serpent?"

"It matters a good deal to me ,"
said Alice hastily;
"but I'm not looking for eggs,
as it happens; and if I was,
I shouldn't want yours :
I don't like them raw."

"Well, be off, then!"
said the Pigeon in a sulky tone,
as it settled down again
into its nest. Alice crouched down
among the trees
as well as she could,
for her neck kept getting
entangled among the branches,
and every now and then
she had to stop and untwist it.
After a while she remembered
that she still held the pieces
of mushroom in her hands,
and she set to work
very carefully,
nibbling first at one
and then at the other,
and growing sometimes taller
and sometimes shorter,
until she had succeeded
in bringing herself
down to her usual height.

It was so long since she had been
anything near the right size,

that it felt quite strange at first;
but she got used to it
in a few minutes,
and began talking to herself,
as usual. "Come,
there's half my plan done now!
How puzzling
all these changes are!
I'm never sure
what I'm going to be,
from one minute to another!
However,
I've got back to my right size:
the next thing is,
to get into that beautiful garden—
how is that to be done,
I wonder?" As she said this,
she came suddenly
upon an open place,
with a little house in it
about four feet high.
"Whoever lives there,"
thought Alice, "it'll never do
to come upon them this size:
why, I should frighten them
out of their wits!"
So she began nibbling
at the righthand bit again,
and did not venture
to go near the house
till she had brought herself
down to nine inches high.

CHAPTER VI.

Pig and Pepper

For a minute or two
she stood looking at the house,
and wondering what to do next,
when suddenly a footman
in livery came running out
of the wood—
(she considered him
to be a footman
because he was in livery:
otherwise,
judging by his face only,
she would have
called him a fish)—
and rapped loudly at the door
with his knuckles.
It was opened by another
footman in livery,
with a round face,
and large eyes like a frog;
and both footmen,
Alice noticed, had powdered hair
that curled all over their heads.
She felt very curious
to know what it was all about,
and crept a little way out of the
wood to listen.

The Fish-Footman began
by producing from under his arm
a great letter,
nearly as large as himself,
and this he handed over
to the other, saying,
in a solemn tone,
"For the Duchess.
An invitation from the Queen
to play croquet."
The Frog-Footman repeated,
in the same solemn tone,
only changing the order
of the words a little,
"From the Queen.
An invitation for the Duchess
to play croquet."

Then they both bowed low,
and their curls
got entangled together.

Alice laughed so much at this,
that she had to run back
into the wood for fear
of their hearing her;
and when she next peeped out
the Fish-Footman was gone,
and the other was sitting
on the ground near the door,
staring stupidly up into the sky.

Alice went timidly up to the door,
and knocked.

"There's no sort of use
in knocking," said the Footman,
"and that for two reasons.
First,
because I'm on the same side
of the door as you are; secondly,
because they're making
such a noise inside,
no one could possibly hear you."
And certainly there was
a most extraordinary noise
going on within—
a constant howling and sneezing,
and every now and then
a great crash,
as if a dish or kettle
had been broken to pieces.

"Please, then," said Alice,
"how am I to get in?"

"There might be some sense

in your knocking,"
the Footman went on
without attending to her,
"if we had the door between us.
For instance, if you were inside ,
you might knock, and
I could let you out, you know."
He was looking up into the sky
all the time he was speaking,
and this Alice
thought decidedly uncivil.
"But perhaps he can't help it,"
she said to herself;
"his eyes are so very nearly
at the top of his head.
But at any rate
he might answer questions.—
How am I to get in?"
she repeated, aloud.

"I shall sit here,"
the Footman remarked,
"till tomorrow—"

At this moment the door
of the house opened,
and a large plate
came skimming out,
straight at the Footman's head:
it just grazed his nose,
and broke to pieces
against one of the trees
behind him.

"—or next day, maybe,"
the Footman continued
in the same tone,
exactly as if nothing
had happened.

"How am I to get in?"
asked Alice again,
in a louder tone.

"Are you to get in at all?"
said the Footman.
"That's the first question,
you know."

It was, no doubt:
only Alice did not like
to be told so.
"It's really dreadful,"
she muttered to herself,
"the way all the creatures argue.
It's enough to drive one crazy!"

The Footman seemed to think
this a good opportunity
for repeating his remark,
with variations.
"I shall sit here," he said,
"on and off, for days and days."

"But what am I to do?" said Alice.

"Anything you like,"
said the Footman,
and began whistling.

"Oh,
there's no use in talking to him,"
said Alice desperately:
"he's perfectly idiotic!"
And she opened the door
and went in.

The door
led right into a large kitchen,
which was full of smoke
from one end to the other:
the Duchess was sitting
on a three-legged stool
in the middle, nursing a baby;
the cook
was leaning over the fire,
stirring a large cauldron
which seemed to be full of soup.

"There's certainly
too much pepper in that soup!"
Alice said to herself,
as well as she could for sneezing.

There was certainly
too much of it in the air.
Even the Duchess
sneezed occasionally;
and as for the baby,
it was sneezing
and howling alternately
without a moment's pause.
The only things
in the kitchen that did not sneeze,
were the cook,
and a large cat which was sitting
on the hearth and grinning
from ear to ear.

"Please would you tell me,"
said Alice, a little timidly,
for she was not quite sure
whether it was good manners
for her to speak first,
"why your cat grins like that?"

"It's a Cheshire cat,"
said the Duchess,
"and that's why. Pig!"

She said the last word
with such sudden violence
that Alice quite jumped;
but she saw in another moment
that it was addressed to the baby,
and not to her,
so she took courage,
and went on again: —

"I didn't know that Cheshire cats
always grinned; in fact,
I didn't know

that cats could grin."

"They all can," said the Duchess;
"and most of 'em do."

"I don't know of any that do,"
Alice said very politely,
feeling quite pleased
to have got into a conversation.

"You don't know much,"
said the Duchess;
"and that's a fact."

Alice did not at all
like the tone of this remark,
and thought it would be as well
to introduce some other subject
of conversation.
While she was trying
to fix on one,
the cook took the cauldron
of soup off the fire,
and at once set to work
throwing everything
within her reach at the Duchess
and the baby —
the fire-irons came first;
then followed a shower
of saucepans, plates, and dishes.
The Duchess took no notice
of them even when they hit her;
and the baby was howling
so much already,
that it was quite impossible to say
whether the blows hurt it or not.

"Oh,
please mind what you're doing!"
cried Alice,
jumping up and down
in an agony of terror. "Oh,
there goes his precious nose!"
as an unusually large saucepan

flew close by it,
and very nearly carried it off.

"If everybody minded
their own business,"
the Duchess said
in a hoarse growl,
"the world would go round
a deal faster than it does."

"Which would not be
an advantage," said Alice,
who felt very glad
to get an opportunity
of showing off
a little of her knowledge.
"Just think of what work
it would make
with the day and night!
You see the earth
takes twenty-four hours
to turn round on its axis—"

"Talking of axes,"
said the Duchess,
"chop off her head!"

Alice glanced
rather anxiously at the cook,
to see if she meant
to take the hint; but the cook
was busily stirring the soup,
and seemed not to be listening,
so she went on again:
"Twenty-four hours,
I think ; or is it twelve? I—"

"Oh, don't bother me,"
said the Duchess;
"I never could abide figures!"
And with that she began
nursing her child again,
singing a sort of lullaby
to it as she did so,

and giving it a violent shake
at the end of every line:

"Speak roughly to your little boy,
    And beat him when he sneezes:
He only does it to annoy,
    Because he knows it teases."

CHORUS.
(In which the cook
and the baby joined):

"Wow! wow! wow!"

While the Duchess sang
the second verse of the song,
she kept tossing the baby
violently up and down,
and the poor little thing
howled so, that Alice
could hardly hear the words:—

"I speak severely to my boy,
    I beat him when he sneezes;
For he can thoroughly enjoy
    The pepper when he pleases!"

CHORUS.

"Wow! wow! wow!"

"Here! you may nurse it a bit,
if you like!"
the Duchess said to Alice,
flinging the baby at her
as she spoke.
"I must go and get ready
to play croquet with the Queen,"
and she hurried out of the room.
The cook threw a frying-pan
after her as she went out,
but it just missed her.

Alice caught the baby

with some difficulty,
as it was a queer-shaped
little creature,
and held out its arms and legs
in all directions,
"just like a star-fish,"
thought Alice.
The poor little thing was snorting
like a steam-engine
when she caught it,
and kept doubling itself up
and straightening itself out again,
so that altogether,
for the first minute or two,
it was as much as she could do
to hold it.

As soon as she had made out
the proper way of nursing it,

(which was to twist it up
into a sort of knot,
and then keep tight hold
of its right ear and left foot,
so as to prevent
its undoing itself,)
she carried it out
into the open air.
"If I don't take
this child away with me,"
thought Alice,
"they're sure to kill it
in a day or two:
wouldn't it be murder
to leave it behind?"
She said the last words out loud,
and the little thing
grunted in reply
(it had left off sneezing
by this time).
"Don't grunt," said Alice;
"that's not at all a proper way
of expressing yourself."

The baby grunted again,
and Alice looked very anxiously
into its face to see
what was the matter with it.
There could be no doubt
that it had a very turn-up nose,
much more like a snout
than a real nose;
also its eyes were getting
extremely small for a baby:
altogether Alice did not like
the look of the thing at all.
"But perhaps
it was only sobbing,"
she thought,
and looked into its eyes again,
to see if there were any tears.

No, there were no tears.
"If you're going to turn into a pig,
my dear," said Alice, seriously,
"I'll have nothing more
to do with you. Mind now!"
The poor little thing sobbed again
(or grunted,
it was impossible to say which),
and they went on
for some while in silence.

Alice was just beginning
to think to herself, "Now,
what am I to do with this creature
when I get it home?"
when it grunted again,
so violently,
that she looked down into its face
in some alarm.
This time there could be
no mistake about it:
it was neither
more nor less than a pig,
and she felt that it would be
quite absurd for her
to carry it further.

So she set
the little creature down,
and felt quite relieved to see it
trot away quietly into the wood.
"If it had grown up,"
she said to herself,
"it would have made
a dreadfully ugly child:
but it makes rather
a handsome pig, I think."
And she began thinking over
other children she knew,
who might do very well as pigs,
and was just saying to herself,
"if one only knew the right way
to change them—"
when she was a little startled
by seeing the Cheshire Cat
sitting on a bough
of a tree a few yards off.

The Cat only grinned
when it saw Alice.
It looked good-natured,
she thought:
still it had very long claws
and a great many teeth,
so she felt that it ought to be
treated with respect.

"Cheshire Puss," she began,
rather timidly,
as she did not at all know
whether it would like the name:
however,
it only grinned a little wider.
"Come, it's pleased so far,"
thought Alice, and she went on.
"Would you tell me, please,
which way I ought to go
from here?"

"That depends a good deal

on where you want to get to,"
said the Cat.

"I don't much care where—"
said Alice.

"Then it doesn't matter
which way you go," said the Cat.

"—so long as I get somewhere ,"
Alice added as an explanation.

"Oh, you're sure to do that,"
said the Cat,
"if you only walk long enough."

Alice felt that this
could not be denied,
so she tried another question.
"What sort of people
 live about here?"

"In that direction," the Cat said,
waving its right paw round,
"lives a Hatter:
and in that direction,"
waving the other paw,
"lives a March Hare.
Visit either you like:
they're both mad."

"But I don't want
to go among mad people,"
Alice remarked.

"Oh, you can't help that,"
said the Cat: "we're all mad here.
I'm mad. You're mad."

"How do you know I'm mad?"
said Alice.

"You must be," said the Cat,
"or you wouldn't have

come here."

Alice didn't think
that proved it at all; however,
she went on "And how do you
know that you're mad?"

"To begin with," said the Cat,
"a dog's not mad.
You grant that?"

"I suppose so," said Alice.

"Well, then," the Cat went on,
"you see,
a dog growls when it's angry,
and wags its tail
when it's pleased.
Now I growl when I'm pleased,
and wag my tail when I'm angry.
Therefore I'm mad."

"I call it purring, not growling,"
said Alice.

"Call it what you like,"
said the Cat.
"Do you play croquet
with the Queen to-day?"

"I should like it very much,"
said Alice,
"but I haven't been invited yet."

"You'll see me there,"
said the Cat, and vanished.

Alice was not much surprised
at this,
she was getting so used
to queer things happening.
While she was looking
at the place where it had been,
it suddenly appeared again.

"By-the-bye,
what became of the baby?"
said the Cat.
"I'd nearly forgotten to ask."

"It turned into a pig,"
Alice quietly said,
just as if it had come back
in a natural way.

"I thought it would,"
said the Cat, and vanished again.

Alice waited a little,
half expecting to see it again,
but it did not appear,
and after a minute or two
she walked on in the direction
in which the March Hare
was said to live.
"I've seen hatters before,"
she said to herself;
"the March Hare will be much
the most interesting,
and perhaps as this is May
it won't be raving mad—
at least not so mad
as it was in March."
As she said this, she looked up,
and there was the Cat again,
sitting on a branch of a tree.

"Did you say pig, or fig?"
said the Cat.

"I said pig," replied Alice;
"and I wish you wouldn't
keep appearing and vanishing
so suddenly:
you make one quite giddy."

"All right," said the Cat;
and this time it vanished

quite slowly,
beginning with the end of the tail,
and ending with the grin,
which remained some time
after the rest of it had gone.

"Well! I've often seen a cat
without a grin," thought Alice;
"but a grin without a cat!
It's the most curious thing
I ever saw in my life!"

She had not gone much farther
before she came in sight
of the house of the March Hare:
she thought it must be
the right house,
because the chimneys
were shaped like ears
and the roof was thatched
with fur. It was so large a house,
that she did not like to go nearer
till she had nibbled some more
of the lefthand bit of mushroom,
and raised herself
to about two feet high:
even then she walked up
towards it rather timidly,
saying to herself
"Suppose it should be
raving mad after all!
I almost wish I'd gone
to see the Hatter instead!"

CHAPTER VII.

A Mad Tea-Party

There was a table set out
under a tree in front of the house,
and the March Hare
and the Hatter
were having tea at it:
a Dormouse was sitting
between them, fast asleep,
and the other two
were using it as a cushion,
resting their elbows on it,
and talking over its head.
"Very uncomfortable
for the Dormouse,"
thought Alice;
"only, as it's asleep,
I suppose it doesn't mind."

The table was a large one,
but the three
were all crowded together
at one corner of it:
"No room! No room!"
they cried out
when they saw Alice coming.
"There's plenty of room!"
said Alice indignantly,
and she sat down
in a large arm-chair
at one end of the table.

"Have some wine,"
the March Hare said
in an encouraging tone.

Alice looked all round the table,
but there was nothing on it
but tea. "I don't see any wine,"
she remarked.

"There isn't any,"

said the March Hare.

"Then it wasn't very civil of you
to offer it," said Alice angrily.

"It wasn't very civil of you
to sit down
without being invited,"
said the March Hare.

"I didn't know it was your table,"
said Alice; "it's laid for
a great many more than three."

"Your hair wants cutting,"
said the Hatter.
He had been looking at Alice
for some time
with great curiosity,
and this was his first speech.

"You should learn not
to make personal remarks,"
Alice said with some severity;
"it's very rude."

The Hatter opened his eyes
very wide on hearing this;
but all he said was,
"Why is a raven
like a writing-desk?"

"Come,
we shall have some fun now!"
thought Alice.
"I'm glad they've begun
asking riddles. —
I believe I can guess that,"
she added aloud.

"Do you mean that you think
you can find out
the answer to it?"
said the March Hare.

"Exactly so," said Alice.

"Then you should say
what you mean,"
the March Hare went on.

"I do," Alice hastily replied;
"at least—
at least I mean what I say—
that's the same thing, you know."

"Not the same thing a bit!"
said the Hatter.
"You might just as well say
that 'I see what I eat'
is the same thing as
 'I eat what I see'!"

"You might just as well say,"
added the March Hare,
"that 'I like what I get' is the
same thing as 'I get what I like'!"

"You might just as well say,"
added the Dormouse,
who seemed to be talking
in his sleep,
"that 'I breathe when I sleep'
is the same thing
as 'I sleep when I breathe'!"

"It is the same thing with you,"
said the Hatter, and here
the conversation dropped,
and the party sat silent
for a minute,
while Alice thought over all
she could remember
about ravens and writing-desks,
which wasn't much.

The Hatter was the first
to break the silence.

"What day of the month is it?"
he said, turning to Alice:
he had taken his watch
out of his pocket,
and was looking at it uneasily,
shaking it every now and then,
and holding it to his ear.

Alice considered a little,
and then said "The fourth."

"Two days wrong!"
sighed the Hatter.
"I told you butter
wouldn't suit the works!"
he added looking angrily
at the March Hare.

"It was the best butter,"
the March Hare meekly replied.

"Yes,
but some crumbs
must have got in as well,"
the Hatter grumbled:
"you shouldn't have put it in
with the bread-knife."

The March Hare took the watch
and looked at it gloomily:
then he dipped it
into his cup of tea,
and looked at it again:
but he could think of nothing
better to say than his first remark,
"It was the best butter,
you know."

Alice had been looking
over his shoulder
with some curiosity.
"What a funny watch!"
she remarked.
"It tells the day of the month,

and doesn't tell
what o'clock it is!"

"Why should it?"
muttered the Hatter.
"Does your watch
tell you what year it is?"

"Of course not,"
Alice replied very readily:
"but that's because
it stays the same year
for such a long time together."

"Which is just the case
with mine," said the Hatter.

Alice felt dreadfully puzzled.
The Hatter's remark
seemed to have no sort
of meaning in it,
and yet it was certainly English.
"I don't quite understand you,"
she said, as politely as she could.

"The Dormouse is asleep again,"
said the Hatter,
and he poured a little hot tea
upon its nose.

The Dormouse
shook its head impatiently,
and said,
without opening its eyes,
"Of course, of course;
just what I was going
to remark myself."

"Have you guessed
the riddle yet?" the Hatter said,
turning to Alice again.

"No, I give it up," Alice replied:
"what's the answer?"

"I haven't the slightest idea,"
said the Hatter.

"Nor I," said the March Hare.

Alice sighed wearily.
"I think you might do something
better with the time," she said,
"than waste it in asking riddles
that have no answers."

"If you knew Time
as well as I do," said the Hatter,
"you wouldn't talk
about wasting it. It's him."

"I don't know what you mean,"
said Alice.

"Of course you don't!"
the Hatter said,
tossing his head contemptuously.
"I dare say you never
even spoke to Time!"

"Perhaps not,"
Alice cautiously replied:
"but I know I have to beat time
when I learn music."

"Ah! that accounts for it,"
said the Hatter.
"He won't stand beating. Now,
if you only kept on good terms
with him,
he'd do almost anything
you liked with the clock.
For instance,
suppose it were nine o'clock
in the morning,
just time to begin lessons:
you'd only have to whisper
a hint to Time,

and round goes the clock
in a twinkling!
Half-past one, time for dinner!"

("I only wish it was,"
the March Hare said to itself
in a whisper.)

"That would be grand, certainly,"
said Alice thoughtfully:
"but then—
I shouldn't be hungry for it,
you know."

"Not at first, perhaps,"
said the Hatter:
"but you could keep it
to half-past one
as long as you liked."

"Is that the way you manage?"
Alice asked.

The Hatter
shook his head mournfully.
"Not I! " he replied.
"We quarrelled last March—
just before he went mad,
you know—"
(pointing with his tea spoon
at the March Hare,)
"—it was at the great concert
given by the Queen of Hearts,
and I had to sing

'Twinkle, twinkle, little bat!

How I wonder what you're at!'

You know the song, perhaps?"

"I've heard something like it,"
said Alice.

"It goes on,you know,"
the Hatter continued,
"in this way:—

'Up above the world you fly,

Like a tea-tray in the sky.

   Twinkle, twinkle—' "

Here the Dormouse shook itself,
and began singing in its sleep
"Twinkle, twinkle, twinkle,
twinkle —" and went on so long
that they had to pinch it
to make it stop.

"Well,
I'd hardly finished
the first verse," said the Hatter,
"when the Queen jumped up
and bawled out,
'He's murdering the time!
Off with his head!' "

"How dreadfully savage!"
exclaimed Alice.

"And ever since that,"
the Hatter went on
in a mournful tone,
"he won't do a thing I ask!
It's always six o'clock now."

A bright idea
came into Alice's head.
"Is that the reason
so many tea-things
are put out here?" she asked.

"Yes, that's it,"
said the Hatter with a sigh:
"it's always tea-time,
and we've no time

to wash the things
between whiles."

"Then you keep moving round,
I suppose?" said Alice.

"Exactly so," said the Hatter:
"as the things get used up."

"But what happens
when you come
to the beginning again?"
Alice ventured to ask.

"Suppose we change the subject,"
the March Hare interrupted,
yawning.
"I'm getting tired of this.
I vote the young lady
tells us a story."

"I'm afraid I don't know one,"
said Alice,
rather alarmed at the proposal.

"Then the Dormouse shall!"
they both cried.
"Wake up, Dormouse!"
And they pinched it
on both sides at once.

The Dormouse
slowly opened his eyes.
"I wasn't asleep,"
he said in a hoarse, feeble voice:
"I heard every word
you fellows were saying."

"Tell us a story!"
said the March Hare.

"Yes, please do!" pleaded Alice.

"And be quick about it,"

added the Hatter,
"or you'll be asleep again
before it's done."

"Once upon a time
there were three little sisters,"
the Dormouse began
in a great hurry;
"and their names were Elsie,
Lacie, and Tillie; and they lived
at the bottom of a well—"

"What did they live on?"
said Alice,
who always took a great interest
in questions of eating
and drinking.

"They lived on treacle,"
said the Dormouse,
after thinking a minute or two.

"They couldn't have done that,
you know,"
Alice gently remarked;
"they'd have been ill."

"So they were,"
said the Dormouse; "very ill."

Alice tried to fancy to herself
what such an extraordinary ways
of living would be like,
but it puzzled her too much,
so she went on:
"But why did they live
at the bottom of a well?"

"Take some more tea,"
the March Hare said to Alice,
very earnestly.

"I've had nothing yet,"
Alice replied

in an offended tone,
"so I can't take more."

"You mean you can't take less,"
said the Hatter: "it's very easy
to take more than nothing."

"Nobody asked your opinion,"
said Alice.

"Who's making
personal remarks now?"
the Hatter asked triumphantly.

Alice did not quite know
what to say to this:
so she helped herself
to some tea and bread-and-butter,
and then turned to the Dormouse,
and repeated her question.
"Why did they live
at the bottom of a well?"

The Dormouse
again took a minute or two
to think about it, and then said,
"It was a treacle-well."

"There's no such thing!"
Alice was beginning very angrily,
but the Hatter
and the March Hare
went "Sh! sh!" and the Dormouse
sulkily remarked,
"If you can't be civil,
you'd better finish the story
for yourself."

"No, please go on!"
Alice said very humbly;
"I won't interrupt again.
I dare say there may be one."

"One, indeed!"

said the Dormouse indignantly.
However, he consented to go on.
"And so these three little sisters—
they were learning to draw,
you know—"

"What did they draw?"
said Alice,
quite forgetting her promise.

"Treacle," said the Dormouse,
without considering at all
this time.

"I want a clean cup,"
interrupted the Hatter:
"let's all move one place on."

He moved on as he spoke,
and the Dormouse followed him:
the March Hare moved
into the Dormouse's place,
and Alice rather unwillingly
took the place of the March Hare.
The Hatter was the only one
who got any advantage
from the change:
and Alice was a good deal
worse off than before,
as the March Hare had just
upset the milk-jug into his plate.

Alice did not wish
to offend the Dormouse again,
so she began very cautiously:
"But I don't understand.
Where did they draw
the treacle from?"

"You can draw water
out of a water-well,"
said the Hatter;
"so I should think you could
draw treacle out

of a treacle-well—eh, stupid?"

"But they were in the well,"
Alice said to the Dormouse,
not choosing
to notice this last remark.

"Of course they were,"
said the Dormouse; "—well in."

This answer
so confused poor Alice,
that she let the Dormouse
go on for some time
without interrupting it.

"They were learning to draw,"
the Dormouse went on,
yawning and rubbing its eyes,
for it was getting very sleepy;
"and they drew
all manner of things—
everything that begins
with an M—"

"Why with an M?" said Alice.

"Why not?" said the March Hare.

Alice was silent.

The Dormouse
had closed its eyes by this time,
and was going off into a doze;
but,
on being pinched by the Hatter,
it woke up again
with a little shriek, and went on:
"—that begins with an M,
such as mouse-traps,
and the moon, and memory,
and muchness—you know
you say things are
"much of a muchness"—

did you ever see such a thing
as a drawing of a muchness?"

"Really, now you ask me,"
said Alice, very much confused,
"I don't think—"

"Then you shouldn't talk,"
said the Hatter.

This piece of rudeness
was more than Alice could bear:
she got up in great disgust,
and walked off; the Dormouse
fell asleep instantly,
and neither of the others
took the least notice of her going,
though she looked back
once or twice,
half hoping that
they would call after her:
the last time she saw them,
they were trying
to put the Dormouse
into the teapot.

"At any rate
I'll never go there again!"
said Alice as she picked her way
through the wood.
"It's the stupidest tea-party
I ever was at in all my life!"

Just as she said this,
she noticed that one of the trees
had a door leading right into it.
"That's very curious!"
she thought.
"But everything's curious today.
I think I may as well go in
at once." And in she went.

Once more she found herself
in the long hall,

and close to the little glass table.
"Now,
I'll manage better this time,"
she said to herself, and began
by taking the little golden key,
and unlocking the door
that led into the garden.
Then she went to work
nibbling at the mushroom
(she had kept
a piece of it in her pocket)
till she was about a foot high:
then she walked down
the little passage:
and then —she found herself
at last in the beautiful garden,
among the bright flower-beds
and the cool fountains.

CHAPTER VIII.

The Queen's
Croquet-Ground

A large rose-tree stood
near the entrance of the garden:
the roses growing on it
were white, but there were
three gardeners at it,
busily painting them red.
Alice thought this
a very curious thing, and
she went nearer to watch them,
and just as she came up to them
she heard one of them say,
"Look out now, Five!
Don't go splashing paint
over me like that!"

"I couldn't help it," said Five,
in a sulky tone;
"Seven jogged my elbow."

On which Seven looked up
and said, "That's right, Five!
Always lay the blame on others!"

"You'd better not talk!" said Five.
"I heard the Queen say
only yesterday
you deserved to be beheaded!"

"What for?" said the one
who had spoken first.

"That's none of your business,
Two!" said Seven.

"Yes, it is his business!" said Five,
"and I'll tell him —
it was for bringing the cook
tulip-roots instead of onions."

Seven flung down his brush,
and had just begun "Well,
of all the unjust things—"
when his eye
chanced to fall upon Alice,
as she stood watching them,
and he checked himself suddenly:
the others looked round also,
and all of them bowed low.

"Would you tell me," said Alice,
a little timidly,
"why you are painting
those roses?"

Five and Seven said nothing,
but looked at Two.
Two began in a low voice,
"Why the fact is, you see, Miss,
this here ought to have been
a red rose-tree,
and we put a white one
in by mistake; and if the Queen
was to find it out,
we should all have
our heads cut off, you know.
So you see, Miss,
we're doing our best,
afore she comes, to—"
At this moment Five,
who had been anxiously
looking across the garden,
called out "The Queen!
The Queen!"
and the three gardeners
instantly threw themselves
flat upon their faces.
There was a sound
of many footsteps,
and Alice looked round,
eager to see the Queen.

First came ten soldiers
carrying clubs;

these were all shaped
like the three gardeners,
oblong and flat,
with their hands
and feet at the corners:
next the ten courtiers;
these were ornamented
all over with diamonds,
and walked two and two,
as the soldiers did.
After these came
the royal children;
there were ten of them,
and the little dears
came jumping merrily along
hand in hand, in couples:
they were all ornamented
with hearts.
Next came the guests,
mostly Kings and Queens,
and among them Alice
recognised the White Rabbit:
it was talking
in a hurried nervous manner,
smiling at everything
that was said, and went by
without noticing her.
Then followed
the Knave of Hearts,
carrying the King's crown
on a crimson velvet cushion;
and,
last of all this grand procession,
came THE KING AND QUEEN
OF HEARTS.

Alice was rather doubtful
whether she ought not
to lie down on her face
like the three gardeners,
but she could not remember
ever having heard
of such a rule at processions;
"and besides,

what would be the use
of a procession," thought she,
"if people had all to lie down
upon their faces,
so that they couldn't see it?"
So she stood still where she was,
and waited.

When the procession
came opposite to Alice,
they all stopped
and looked at her, and the Queen
said severely "Who is this?"
She said it to the Knave of Hearts,
who only bowed
and smiled in reply.

"Idiot!" said the Queen,
tossing her head impatiently;
and, turning to Alice,
she went on,
"What's your name, child?"

"My name is Alice,
so please your Majesty,"
said Alice very politely;
but she added, to herself, "Why,
they're only a pack of cards,
after all.
I needn't be afraid of them!"

"And who are these?"
said the Queen,
pointing to the three gardeners
who were lying round
the rose-tree; for, you see,
as they were lying on their faces,
and the pattern on their backs
was the same
as the rest of the pack,
she could not tell
whether they were gardeners,
or soldiers, or courtiers,
or three of her own children.

"How should I know?"
said Alice,
surprised at her own courage.
"It's no business of mine."

The Queen
turned crimson with fury, and,
after glaring at her for a moment
like a wild beast, screamed
"Off with her head! Off—"

"Nonsense!" said Alice,
very loudly and decidedly,
and the Queen was silent.

The King laid his hand
upon her arm,
and timidly said
"Consider, my dear:
she is only a child!"

The Queen
turned angrily away from him,
and said to the Knave
"Turn them over!"

The Knave did so,
very carefully, with one foot.

"Get up!" said the Queen,
in a shrill, loud voice,
and the three gardeners
instantly jumped up,
and began bowing to the King,
the Queen, the royal children,
and everybody else.

"Leave off that!"
screamed the Queen.
"You make me giddy." And then,
turning to the rose-tree,
she went on,
"What have you

been doing here?"

"May it please your Majesty,"
said Two, in a very humble tone,
going down on one knee
as he spoke, "we were trying—"

"I see!" said the Queen,
who had meanwhile
been examining the roses.
"Off with their heads!"
and the procession moved on,
three of the soldiers
remaining behind to execute
the unfortunate gardeners,
who ran to Alice for protection.

"You shan't be beheaded!"
said Alice,
and she put them
into a large flower-pot
that stood near.
The three soldiers
wandered about
for a minute or two,
looking for them,
and then quietly marched off
after the others.

"Are their heads off?"
shouted the Queen.

"Their heads are gone,
if it please your Majesty!"
the soldiers shouted in reply.

"That's right!"
shouted the Queen.
"Can you play croquet?"

The soldiers were silent,
and looked at Alice,
as the question
was evidently meant for her.

"Yes!" shouted Alice.

"Come on, then!"
roared the Queen,
and Alice joined the procession,
wondering very much
what would happen next.

"It's—it's a very fine day!"
said a timid voice at her side.
She was walking
by the White Rabbit,
who was peeping
anxiously into her face.

"Very," said Alice:
"—where's the Duchess?"

"Hush! Hush!"
said the Rabbit in a low,
hurried tone.
He looked anxiously
over his shoulder as he spoke,
and then raised himself
upon tiptoe,
put his mouth close to her ear,
and whispered
"She's under sentence
of execution."

"What for?" said Alice.

"Did you say 'What a pity!'?"
the Rabbit asked.

"No, I didn't," said Alice:
"I don't think it's at all a pity.
I said 'What for?' "

"She boxed the Queen's ears—"
the Rabbit began. Alice
gave a little scream of laughter.
"Oh, hush!" the Rabbit whispered
in a frightened tone.
"The Queen will hear you!
You see, she came rather late,
and the Queen said—"

"Get to your places!"
shouted the Queen
in a voice of thunder,
and people began running
about in all directions,
tumbling up against each other;
however,
they got settled down
in a minute or two,
and the game began.
Alice thought she had never seen
such a curious croquet-ground
in her life;
it was all ridges and furrows;
the balls were live hedgehogs,
the mallets live flamingoes,
and the soldiers
had to double themselves up
and to stand on their hands
and feet, to make the arches.

The chief difficulty
Alice found at first
was in managing her flamingo:
she succeeded
in getting its body tucked away,
comfortably enough,
under her arm,
with its legs hanging down,
but generally,
just as she had got its neck
nicely straightened out,
and was going to give
the hedgehog a blow
with its head,
it would twist itself round
and look up in her face,
with such a puzzled expression
that she could not help

bursting out laughing:
and when she had
got its head down,
and was going to begin again,
it was very provoking to find
that the hedgehog
had unrolled itself,
and was in the act
of crawling away: besides all this,
there was generally a ridge
or furrow in the way
wherever she wanted
to send the hedgehog to, and,
as the doubled-up soldiers
were always getting up
and walking off
to other parts of the ground,
Alice soon came to the conclusion
that it was
a very difficult game indeed.

The players all played at once
without waiting for turns,
quarrelling all the while,
and fighting for the hedgehogs;
and in a very short time
the Queen
was in a furious passion,
and went stamping about,
and shouting "Off with his head!"
or "Off with her head!"
about once in a minute.

Alice began to feel very uneasy:
to be sure,
she had not as yet
had any dispute with the Queen,
but she knew
that it might happen any minute,
"and then," thought she,
"what would become of me?
They're dreadfully
fond of beheading people here;
the great wonder is,

that there's any one left alive!"

She was looking about
for some way of escape,
and wondering whether
she could get away
without being seen,
when she noticed
a curious appearance in the air:
it puzzled her very much at first,
but,
after watching it a minute or two,
she made it out to be a grin,
and she said to herself
"It's the Cheshire Cat:
now I shall have somebody
to talk to."

"How are you getting on?"
said the Cat,
as soon as there was mouth
enough for it to speak with.

Alice waited
till the eyes appeared,
and then nodded.
"It's no use speaking to it,"
she thought,
"till its ears have come,
or at least one of them."
In another minute
the whole head appeared,
and then Alice
put down her flamingo,
and began an account
of the game,
feeling very glad
she had someone to listen to her.
The Cat seemed to think
that there was enough of it
now in sight,
and no more of it appeared.

"I don't think they play

at all fairly," Alice began,
in rather a complaining tone,
"and they all quarrel
so dreadfully
one can't hear oneself speak—
and they don't seem
to have any rules in particular;
at least, if there are,
nobody attends to them—
and you've no idea
how confusing it is
all the things being alive;
for instance, there's the arch
I've got to go through next
walking about at the other end
of the ground—
and I should have croqueted
the Queen's hedgehog just now,
only it ran away
when it saw mine coming!"

"How do you like the Queen?"
said the Cat in a low voice.

"Not at all," said Alice:
"she's so extremely—"
Just then she noticed
that the Queen
was close behind her, listening:
so she went on,"—likely to win,
that it's hardly worth while
finishing the game."

The Queen smiled and passed on.

"Who are you talking to?"
said the King, going up to Alice,
and looking at the Cat's head
with great curiosity.

"It's a friend of mine—
a Cheshire Cat," said Alice:
"allow me to introduce it."

"I don't like the look of it at all,"
said the King: "however,
it may kiss my hand if it likes."

"I'd rather not,"
the Cat remarked.

"Don't be impertinent,"
said the King,
"and don't look at me like that!"
He got behind Alice as he spoke.

"A cat may look at a king,"
said Alice.
"I've read that in some book,
but I don't remember where.
"

"Well, it must be removed,"
said the King very decidedly,
and he called the Queen,
who was passing at the moment,
"My dear!
I wish you would have
this cat removed!"

The Queen had only one way
of settling all difficulties,
great or small.
"Off with his head!" she said,
without even looking round.

"I'll fetch the executioner myself,"
said the King eagerly,
and he hurried off.

Alice thought
she might as well go back,
and see how the game
was going on,
as she heard the Queen's voice
in the distance,
screaming with passion.
She had already heard her

sentence three of the players
to be executed
for having missed their turns,
and she did not like the look
of things at all, as the game
was in such confusion
that she never knew
whether it was her turn or not.
So she went in search
of her hedgehog.

The hedgehog was engaged
in a fight with another hedgehog,
which seemed to Alice
an excellent opportunity
for croqueting one of them
with the other:
the only difficulty was,
that her flamingo was gone across
to the other side of the garden,
where Alice could see it
trying in a helpless sort of way
to fly up into a tree.

By the time she had caught
the flamingo and brought it back,
the fight was over,
and both the hedgehogs
were out of sight:
"but it doesn't matter much,"
thought Alice,
"as all the arches are gone
from this side of the ground."
So she tucked it away
under her arm,
that it might not escape again,
and went back
for a little more conversation
with her friend.

When she got back
to the Cheshire Cat,
she was surprised to find
quite a large crowd

collected round it:
there was a dispute
going on between
the executioner, the King,
and the Queen,
who were all talking at once,
while all the rest
were quite silent,
and looked very uncomfortable.

The moment Alice appeared,
she was appealed to by all three
to settle the question,
and they repeated
their arguments to her, though,
as they all spoke at once,
she found it very hard indeed
to make out exactly
what they said.

The executioner's argument was,
that you couldn't cut off a head
unless there was a body
to cut it off from:
that he had never had to do
such a thing before,
and he wasn't going
to begin at his time of life.

The King's argument was,
that anything that had a head
could be beheaded,
and that you weren't
to talk nonsense.

The Queen's argument was,
that if something
wasn't done about it
in less than no time
she'd have everybody executed,
all round.

(It was this last remark that had
made the whole party

look so grave and anxious.)

Alice
could think of nothing else to say
but "It belongs to the Duchess:
you'd better ask her about it."

"She's in prison," the Queen said
to the executioner:
"fetch her here."
And the executioner
went off like an arrow.

The Cat's head
began fading away
the moment he was gone, and,
by the time he had come back
with the Duchess,
it had entirely disappeared;
so the King and the executioner
ran wildly up and down
looking for it,
while the rest of the party
went back to the game.

CHAPTER IX.

The Mock Turtle's Story

"You can't think how glad
I am to see you again,
you dear old thing!"
said the Duchess,
as she tucked her arm
affectionately into Alice's,
and they walked off together.

Alice was very glad to find her
in such a pleasant temper,
and thought to herself
that perhaps it was only
the pepper that had made her
so savage when they met
in the kitchen.

"When I'm a Duchess,"
she said to herself,

(not in a very hopeful tone
though),
"I won't have any pepper
in my kitchen at all .
Soup does very well without—
Maybe it's always pepper
that makes people
hot-tempered," she went on,
very much pleased at having
found out a new kind of rule,
"and vinegar
that makes them sour—
and camomile
that makes them bitter—and—
and barley-sugar and such things
that make children
sweet-tempered.
I only wish people knew that :
then they wouldn't be
so stingy about it, you know—"

She had quite forgotten
the Duchess by this time,
and was a little startled
when she heard her voice
 close to her ear.
"You're thinking
about something, my dear,
and that makes you forget to talk.
I can't tell you just now
what the moral of that is,
but I shall remember it in a bit."

"Perhaps it hasn't one,"
Alice ventured to remark.

"Tut, tut, child!"
said the Duchess.
"Everything's got a moral,
if only you can find it." And she
squeezed herself up closer
to Alice's side as she spoke.

Alice did not much like
keeping so close to her: first,
because the Duchess
was very ugly; and secondly,
because she was exactly
the right height to rest her chin
upon Alice's shoulder,
and it was an uncomfortably
sharp chin. However,
she did not like to be rude,
so she bore it as well as she could.

"The game's going on
rather better now," she said,
by way of keeping up
the conversation a little.

"'Tis so," said the Duchess:
"and the moral of that is—
 'Oh, 'tis love, 'tis love,
that makes the world go round!' "

"Somebody said,"
Alice whispered,
"that it's done by everybody
minding their own business!"

"Ah, well!
It means much the same thing,"
said the Duchess,
digging her sharp little chin
into Alice's shoulder
as she added,
"and the moral of that is—
 'Take care of the sense,
and the sounds will take care
of themselves.' "

"How fond she is
of finding morals in things!"
Alice thought to herself.

"I dare say you're wondering
why I don't put my arm
round your waist,"
the Duchess said after a pause:
"the reason is,
that I'm doubtful about
the temper of your flamingo.
Shall I try the experiment?"

"He might bite,"
Alice cautiously replied,
not feeling at all anxious
to have the experiment tried.

"Very true," said the Duchess:
"flamingoes
and mustard both bite.
And the moral of that is—
 'Birds of a feather
flock together.' "

"Only mustard isn't a bird,"
Alice remarked.

"Right, as usual,"
said the Duchess:
"what a clear way
you have of putting things!"

"It's a mineral, I think ,"
said Alice.

"Of course it is,"
said the Duchess,
who seemed ready to agree
to everything that Alice said;
"there's a large
mustard-mine near here.
And the moral of that is—
 'The more there is of mine,
the less there is of yours.' "

"Oh, I know!" exclaimed Alice,
who had not attended
to this last remark,
"it's a vegetable.
It doesn't look like one, but it is."

"I quite agree with you,"
said the Duchess;
"and the moral of that is—
 'Be what you
would seem to be'—
or if you'd like it
put more simply—
 'Never imagine yourself
not to be otherwise
than what it might
appear to others
that what you were
or might have been
was not otherwise
than what you had been
would have appeared to them
to be otherwise.' "

"I think I should understand
that better,"

Alice said very politely,
"if I had it written down:
but I can't quite follow it
as you say it."

"That's nothing
to what I could say if I chose,"
the Duchess replied,
in a pleased tone.

"Pray don't trouble yourself
to say it any longer than that,"
said Alice.

"Oh, don't talk about trouble!"
said the Duchess.
"I make you a present
of everything I've said as yet."

"A cheap sort of present!"
thought Alice.
"I'm glad they don't give
birthday presents like that!"
But she did not venture
to say it out loud.

"Thinking again?"
the Duchess asked,
with another dig
of her sharp little chin.

"I've a right to think,"
said Alice sharply,
for she was beginning
to feel a little worried.

"Just about as much right,"
said the Duchess,
"as pigs have to fly; and the m—"

But here, to Alice's great surprise,
the Duchess's voice died away,
even in the middle
of her favourite word 'moral,

'and the arm that was linked
into hers began to tremble.
Alice looked up,
and there stood the Queen
in front of them,
with her arms folded,
frowning like a thunderstorm.

"A fine day, your Majesty!"
the Duchess began in a low,
weak voice.

"Now, I give you fair warning,"
shouted the Queen,
stamping on the ground
as she spoke;
"either you or your head
must be off,
and that in about half no time!
Take your choice!"

The Duchess took her choice,
and was gone in a moment.

"Let's go on with the game,"
the Queen said to Alice;
and Alice
was too much frightened
to say a word,
but slowly followed her
back to the croquet-ground.

The other guests
had taken advantage
of the Queen's absence,
and were resting in the shade:
however,
the moment they saw her,
they hurried back to the game,
the Queen merely remarking that
a moment's delay
would cost them their lives.

All the time they were playing

the Queen
never left off quarrelling
with the other players,
and shouting "Off with his head!"
or "Off with her head!"
Those whom she sentenced
were taken into custody
by the soldiers,
who of course had to
leave off being arches to do this,
so that by the end of half an hour
or so there were no arches left,
and all the players,
except the King, the Queen,
and Alice, were in custody
and under sentence of execution.

Then the Queen left off,
quite out of breath,
and said to Alice, "Have you seen
the Mock Turtle yet?"

"No, " said Alice.
"I don't even know
what a Mock Turtle is."

"It's the thing
Mock Turtle Soup is made from,"
said the Queen.

"I never saw one,
or heard of one," said Alice.

"Come on, then," said the Queen,
"and he shall tell you
his history,"

As they walked off together,
Alice heard
the King say in a low voice,
to the company generally,
"You are all pardoned."
"Come, that's a good thing!"
she said to herself,

for she had felt quite unhappy
at the number of executions
the Queen had ordered.

They very soon came upon
a Gryphon,
lying fast asleep in the sun.

(If you don't know what
a Gryphon is, look at the picture.)
"Up, lazy thing!" said the Queen,
"and take this young lady
to see the Mock Turtle,
and to hear his history.
I must go back and see
after some executions
I have ordered;"
and she walked off,
leaving Alice alone
with the Gryphon.
Alice did not quite like the look
of the creature, but on the whole
she thought it would be
quite as safe to stay with it
as to go after that savage Queen:
so she waited.

The Gryphon sat up
and rubbed its eyes:
then it watched the Queen
till she was out of sight:
then it chuckled.
"What fun!" said the Gryphon,
half to itself, half to Alice.

"What is the fun?" said Alice.

"Why, she," said the Gryphon.
"It's all her fancy, that:
they never executes nobody,
you know. Come on!"

"Everybody says
'come on!' here,"

thought Alice,
as she went slowly after it:
"I never was so ordered about
in all my life, never!"

They had not gone far
before they saw
the Mock Turtle in the distance,
sitting sad and lonely
on a little ledge of rock, and,
as they came nearer,
Alice could hear him sighing
as if his heart would break.
She pitied him deeply.
"What is his sorrow?"
she asked the Gryphon,
and the Gryphon answered,
very nearly
in the same words as before,
"It's all his fancy, that:
he hasn't got no sorrow,
you know. Come on!"

So they went up
to the Mock Turtle,
who looked at them
with large eyes full of tears,
but said nothing.

"This here young lady,"
said the Gryphon,
"she wants for to know
your history, she do."

"I'll tell it her,"
said the Mock Turtle in a deep,
hollow tone:
"sit down, both of you,
and don't speak a word
till I've finished."

So they sat down,
and nobody spoke
for some minutes.

Alice thought to herself,
"I don't see
how he can ever finish,
if he doesn't begin."
But she waited patiently.

"Once,"
said the Mock Turtle at last,
with a deep sigh,
"I was a real Turtle."

These words were followed
by a very long silence,
broken only by
an occasional exclamation
of "Hjckrrh!" from the Gryphon,
and the constant heavy sobbing
of the Mock Turtle.
Alice was very nearly
getting up and saying,
"Thank you, sir,
for your interesting story,"
but she could not help thinking
there must be more to come,
so she sat still and said nothing.

"When we were little,"
the Mock Turtle went on at last,
more calmly,
though still sobbing
a little now and then,
"we went to school in the sea.
The master was an old Turtle—
we used to call him Tortoise—"

"Why did you call him Tortoise,
if he wasn't one?" Alice asked.

"We called him Tortoise
because he taught us,"
said the Mock Turtle angrily:
"really you are very dull!"

"You ought to be ashamed

of yourself for asking
such a simple question,"
added the Gryphon;
and then they both sat silent
and looked at poor Alice, who
felt ready to sink into the earth.
At last the Gryphon
said to the Mock Turtle,
"Drive on, old fellow!
Don't be all day about it!"
and he went on in these words:

"Yes,
we went to school in the sea,
though you mayn't believe it—"

"I never said I didn't!"
interrupted Alice.

"You did," said the Mock Turtle.

"Hold your tongue!"
added the Gryphon,
before Alice could speak again.
The Mock Turtle went on.

"We had the best of educations—
in fact,
we went to school every day—"

"I've been to a day-school, too,"
said Alice; "you needn't be
so proud as all that."

"With extras?"
asked the Mock Turtle
a little anxiously.

"Yes," said Alice,
"we learned French and music."

"And washing?"
said the Mock Turtle.

"Certainly not!"
said Alice indignantly.

"Ah! then yours
wasn't a really good school,"
said the Mock Turtle
in a tone of great relief.
"Now at ours they had
at the end of the bill,
'French, music,
and washing —extra.' "

"You couldn't have
wanted it much," said Alice;
"living at the bottom of the sea."

"I couldn't afford to learn it."
said the Mock Turtle with a sigh.
"I only took the regular course."

"What was that?" inquired Alice.

"Reeling and Writhing,
of course, to begin with,"
the Mock Turtle replied;
"and then the different branches
of Arithmetic—
Ambition, Distraction,
Uglification, and Derision."

"I never heard of 'Uglification,' "
Alice ventured to say.
"What is it?"

The Gryphon lifted up
both its paws in surprise. "What!
Never heard of uglifying!"
it exclaimed.
"You know what to beautify is,
I suppose?"

"Yes," said Alice doubtfully:
"it means—to—make—
anything—prettier."

"Well, then,"
the Gryphon went on,
"if you don't know
what to uglify is,
you are a simpleton."

Alice did not feel encouraged
to ask any more questions
about it,
so she turned to the Mock Turtle,
and said
"What else had you to learn?"

"Well, there was Mystery,"
the Mock Turtle replied,
counting off the subjects
on his flappers," —
Mystery, ancient and modern,
with Seaography:
then Drawling — the Dra**wling-**
master was an old conger-eel,
that used to come once a week:
 he taught us Drawling,
Stretching, and Fainting in Coils."

"What was that like?" said Alice.

"Well,
I can't show it you myself,"
the Mock Turtle said:
"I'm too stiff.
And the Gryphon
never learnt it."

"Hadn't time," said the Gryphon:
"I went to the Classics master,
though.
He was an old crab, he was."

"I never went to him,"
the Mock Turtle said with a sigh:
"he taught Laughing and Grief,
they used to say."

"So he did, so he did,"
said the Gryphon,
sighing in his turn;
and both creatures
hid their faces in their paws.

"And how many hours
a day did you do lessons?"
said Alice,
in a hurry to change the subject.

"Ten hours the first day,"
said the Mock Turtle:
"nine the next, and so on."

"What a curious plan!"
exclaimed Alice.

"That's the reason
they're called lessons,"
the Gryphon remarked:
"because they lessen
from day to day."

This was quite a new idea
to Alice,
and she thought it over a little
before she made her next remark.
"Then the eleventh day
must have been a holiday?"

"Of course it was,"
said the Mock Turtle.

"And how did you manage
on the twelfth?"
Alice went on eagerly.

"That's enough about lessons,"
the Gryphon interrupted
in a very decided tone:
"tell her something about
the games now."

CHAPTER X.

The Lobster Quadrille

The Mock Turtle sighed deeply,
and drew the back
of one flapper across his eyes.
He looked at Alice,
and tried to speak,
but for a minute
or two sobs choked his voice.
"Same as if he had a bone
in his throat," said the Gryphon:
and it set to work shaking him
and punching him in the back.
At last the Mock Turtle
recovered his voice,
and, with tears
running down his cheeks,
he went on again:—

"You may not have lived
much under the sea—"
("I haven't, " said Alice)—
"and perhaps you were never
even introduced to a lobster—"
(Alice began to say
"I once tasted—"
but checked herself hastily,
and said "No, never") "—
so you can have no idea
what a delightful thing
a Lobster Quadrille is!"

"No, indeed," said Alice.
"What sort of a dance is it?"

"Why, " said the Gryphon,
"you first form into a line
along the sea-shore—"

"Two lines!"
cried the Mock Turtle.
"Seals, turtles,

salmon, and so on; then,
when you've cleared
all the jelly-fish out of the way—"

"That generally
takes some time,"
interrupted the Gryphon.

"—you advance twice—"

"Each with a lobster
as a partner!" cried the Gryphon.

"Of course,"
the Mock Turtle said:
"advance twice, set to partners—"

"—change lobsters,
and retire in same order,"
continued the Gryphon.

"Then, you know,"
the Mock Turtle went on,
"you throw the—"

"The lobsters!"
shouted the Gryphon,
with a bound into the air.

"—as far out to sea as you can—"

"Swim after them!"
screamed the Gryphon.

"Turn a somersault in the sea!"
cried the Mock Turtle,
capering wildly about.

"Change lobsters again!"
yelled the Gryphon
at the top of its voice.

"Back to land again,
and that's all the first figure,

" said the Mock Turtle,
suddenly dropping his voice;
and the two creatures,
who had been jumping about
like mad things all this time,
sat down again very sadly
and quietly, and looked at Alice.

"It must be a very pretty dance,"
said Alice timidly.

"Would you like to see
a little of it?"
said the Mock Turtle.

"Very much indeed," said Alice.

"Come, let's try the first figure!"
said the Mock Turtle
to the Gryphon.
"We can do without lobsters,
you know. Which shall sing?"

"Oh, you sing,"
said the Gryphon.
"I've forgotten the words."

So they began solemnly
dancing round and round Alice,
every now and then
treading on her toes
when they passed too close,
and waving their forepaws
to mark the time,
while the Mock Turtle sang this,
very slowly and sadly:—

"Will you walk a little faster?"
said a whiting to a snail.
"There's a porpoise
close behind us,
and he's treading on my tail.
See how eagerly the lobsters
and the turtles all advance!

They are waiting on the shingle—
will you come and join the dance?
Will you, won't you,
will you, won't you,
will you join the dance?
Will you, won't you,
will you, won't you,
won't you join the dance?

"You can really have no notion
how delightful it will be When
they take us up and throw us,
with the lobsters, out to sea!"
But the snail replied
"Too far, too far!"
and gave a look askance—
Said he thanked
the whiting kindly,
but he would not join the dance.
Would not, could not,
would not, could not,
would not join the dance.
Would not, could not,
would not, could not,
could not join the dance.

"What matters it how far we go?"
his scaly friend replied.
"There is another shore,
you know, upon the other side.
The further off from England
the nearer is to France—
Then turn not pale, beloved snail,
but come and join the dance.
Will you, won't you,
will you, won't you,
will you join the dance?
Will you, won't you,
will you, won't you,
won't you join the dance?"

"Thank you,
it's a very interesting dance

to watch," said Alice,
feeling very glad
that it was over at last:
"and I do so like
that curious song
about the whiting!"

"Oh, as to the whiting,"
said the Mock Turtle,
"they—you've seen them,
of course?"

"Yes," said Alice,
"I've often seen them at dinn—"
she checked herself hastily.

"I don't know
where Dinn may be,"
said the Mock Turtle,
"but if you've seen them so often,
of course you know
what they're like."

"I believe so,"
Alice replied thoughtfully.
"They have their tails
in their mouths—
and they're all over crumbs."

"You're wrong
about the crumbs,"
said the Mock Turtle:
"crumbs would all wash off
in the sea.
But they have their tails
in their mouths;
and the reason is—"
here the Mock Turtle yawned
and shut his eyes. —
"Tell her about the reason
and all that,"
he said to the Gryphon.

"The reason is,"

said the Gryphon,
"that they would go
with the lobsters to the dance.
So they got thrown out to sea.
So they had to fall a long way.
So they got their tails fast
in their mouths.
So they couldn't get them
out again. That's all."

"Thank you," said Alice,
"it's very interesting.
I never knew so much
about a whiting before.
"

"I can tell you more than that,
if you like," said the Gryphon.
"Do you know
why it's called a whiting?"

"I never thought about it,"
said Alice. "Why?"

"It does the boots and shoes,."
the Gryphon replied
very solemnly.

Alice was thoroughly puzzled.
"Does the boots and shoes!."
she repeated in a wondering tone.

"Why,
what are your shoes done with?"
said the Gryphon. "I mean,
what makes them so shiny? "

Alice looked down at them,
and considered a little
before she gave her answer.
"They're done with blacking,
I believe."

"Boots and shoes under the sea,"

the Gryphon went on
in a deep voice,
"are done with a whiting.
Now you know."

"And what are they made of?"
Alice asked
in a tone of great curiosity.

"Soles and eels, of course,"
the Gryphon replied
rather impatiently:
"any shrimp
could have told you that."

"If I'd been the whiting,"
said Alice,
whose thoughts
were still running on the song,
"I'd have said to the porpoise,
 'Keep back, please:
we don't want you with us!' "

"They were obliged
to have him with them,"
the Mock Turtle said:
"no wise fish would go anywhere
without a porpoise."

"Wouldn't it really?" said Alice
in a tone of great surprise.

"Of course not,"
said the Mock Turtle: "why,
if a fish came to me ,
and told me
he was going a journey,
I should say
 'With what porpoise?' "

"Don't you mean 'purpose'?"
said Alice.

"I mean what I say,"

the Mock Turtle replied
in an offended tone.
And the Gryphon added
"Come, let's hear
some of your adventures."

"I could tell you my adventures—
beginning from this morning,"
said Alice a little timidly:
"but it's no use
going back to yesterday, because
I was a different person then."

"Explain all that,"
said the Mock Turtle.

"No, no!
The adventures first,"
said the Gryphon
in an impatient tone:
"explanations
take such a dreadful time."

So Alice began telling them
her adventures from the time
when she first saw
the White Rabbit.
She was a little nervous
about it just at first,
the two creatures
got so close to her,
one on each side,
and opened their eyes
and mouths so very wide,
but she gained courage
as she went on.
Her listeners were perfectly quiet
till she got to the part about her
repeating "You are old,
Father William ,"
to the Caterpillar,
and the words
all coming different,
and then the Mock Turtle

drew a long breath,
and said "That's very curious."

"It's all about as curious
as it can be," said the Gryphon.

"It all came different!"
the Mock Turtle
repeated thoughtfully.
"I should like to hear her try
and repeat something now.
Tell her to begin."
He looked at the Gryphon
as if he thought it had some kind
of authority over Alice.

"Stand up and repeat ''
Tis the voice of the sluggard,' "
said the Gryphon.

"How the creatures
order one about,
and make one repeat lessons!"
thought Alice;
"I might as well be at school
at once." However, she got up,
and began to repeat it,
but her head was so full
of the Lobster Quadrille,
that she hardly knew
what she was saying,
and the words
came very queer indeed:—

"'Tis the voice of the Lobster;
I heard him declare,
"You have baked me too brown,
I must sugar my hair."
As a duck with its eyelids,
so he with his nose
Trims his belt and his buttons,
and turns out his toes."

When the sands are all dry,

he is gay as a lark,
And will talk
in contemptuous tones
of the Shark,
But, when the tide rises
and sharks are around,
His voice has a timid
and tremulous sound.

"That's different
from what I used to say
when I was a child,"
said the Gryphon.

"Well,
I never heard it before,"
said the Mock Turtle;
"but it sounds
uncommon nonsense."

Alice said nothing;
she had sat down
with her face in her hands,
wondering if anything
would ever happen
in a natural way again.

"I should like to have it
explained," said the Mock Turtle.

"She can't explain it,"
said the Gryphon hastily.
"Go on with the next verse."

"But about his toes?"
the Mock Turtle persisted.
"How could he turn them out
with his nose, you know?"

"It's the first position in dancing."
Alice said;
but was dreadfully puzzled
by the whole thing,

and longed to change the subject.

"Go on with the next verse,"
the Gryphon
repeated impatiently: "it begins
' I passed by his garden .' "

Alice did not dare to disobey,
though she felt sure
it would all come wrong,
and she went on
in a trembling voice:—

"I passed by his garden,
and marked,
with one eye,

How the Owl and the Panther
were sharing a pie—"

The Panther took pie-crust,
and gravy, and meat,

While the Owl had the dish
as its share of the treat.

When the pie was all finished,
the Owl, as a boon,

Was kindly permitted
to pocket the spoon:

While the Panther received
knife and fork with a growl,

And concluded the banquet—

"What is the use
of repeating all that stuff,"
the Mock Turtle interrupted,
"if you don't explain it
as you go on?
It's by far the most
confusing thing I ever heard!"

"Yes,
I think you'd better leave off,"
said the Gryphon: and Alice
was only too glad to do so.

"Shall we try another figure
of the Lobster Quadrille?"
the Gryphon went on.
"Or would you like
the Mock Turtle
to sing you a song?"

"Oh, a song, please,
if the Mock Turtle
would be so kind," Alice replied,
so eagerly that the Gryphon said,
in a rather offended tone,
"Hm! No accounting for tastes!
Sing her ' Turtle Soup,'
will you, old fellow?"

The Mock Turtle sighed deeply,
and began,
in a voice sometimes
choked with sobs, to sing this:—

"Beautiful Soup,
so rich and green,
Waiting in a hot tureen!
Who for such dainties
would not stoop?
Soup of the evening,
beautiful Soup!
Soup of the evening,
beautiful Soup!

Beau—ootiful Soo—oop!
Beau—ootiful Soo—oop!
Soo—oop of the e—e—evening,
Beautiful, beautiful Soup!

"Beautiful Soup!
Who cares for fish,

Game, or any other dish?
Who would not give all else
for two pennyworth
only of beautiful Soup?
Pennyworth
only of beautiful Soup?
        Beau—ootiful Soo—oop!
        Beau—ootiful Soo—oop!
Soo—oop of the e—e—evening,
   Beautiful, beauti—FUL SOUP!"

"Chorus again!"
cried the Gryphon,
and the Mock Turtle
had just begun to repeat it,
when a cry of
"The trial's beginning!"
was heard in the distance.

"Come on!" cried the Gryphon,
and, taking Alice by the hand,
it hurried off, without waiting
for the end of the song.

"What trial is it?"
Alice panted as she ran;
but the Gryphon only answered
"Come on!" and ran the faster,
while more and more
faintly came,
carried on the breeze
that followed them,
the melancholy words:—

"Soo—oop of the e—e—evening,
      Beautiful, beautiful Soup!"

CHAPTER XI.

Who Stole the Tarts?

The King and Queen of Hearts
were seated on their throne
when they arrived,
with a great crowd
assembled about them—
all sorts of little birds and beasts,
as well as
the whole pack of cards:
the Knave
was standing before them,
in chains,
with a soldier
on each side to guard him;
and near the King
was the White Rabbit,
with a trumpet in one hand,
and a scroll of parchment
in the other.
In the very middle
of the court was a table,
with a large dish of tarts upon it:
they looked so good,
that it made Alice
quite hungry to look at them—
"I wish they'd get the trial done,"
she thought,"
and hand round
the refreshments!"
But there seemed
to be no chance of this,
so she began
looking at everything about her,
to pass away the time.

Alice had never been
in a court of justice before,
but she had read about them
in books,
and she was quite pleased
to find that she knew the name
of nearly everything there.
"That's the judge,"
she said to herself,
"because of his great wig."

The judge, by the way,
was the King;
and as he wore his crown
over the wig,

(look at the frontispiece
if you want to see how he did it,)
he did not look at all comfortable,
and it was certainly
not becoming.

"And that's the jury-box,"
thought Alice,
"and those twelve creatures,"
(she was obliged to say
"creatures," you see,
because some of them
were animals,
and some were birds,) "
I suppose they are the jurors."
She said this last word
two or three times over to herself,
being rather proud of it:
for she thought, and rightly too,
that very few little girls of her age
knew the meaning of it at all.
However, "jury-men"
would have done just as well.

The twelve jurors were all writing
very busily on slates.
"What are they doing?"
Alice whispered to the Gryphon.
"They can't have anything
to put down yet,
before the trial's begun."

"They're putting down
their names," the Gryphon

whispered in reply,
"for fear they should forget them
before the end of the trial."

"Stupid things!"
Alice began in a loud,
indignant voice,
but she stopped hastily,
for the White Rabbit cried out,
"Silence in the court!"
and the King
put on his spectacles
and looked anxiously round,
to make out who was talking.

Alice could see,
as well as if she were looking
over their shoulders,
that all the jurors
were writing down
"stupid things!" on their slates,
and she could even make out
that one of them didn't know
how to spell "stupid,"
and that he had to ask
his neighbour to tell him.
"A nice muddle their slates'll
be in before the trial's over!"
thought Alice.

One of the jurors
had a pencil that squeaked.
This of course,
Alice could not stand,
and she went round the court
and got behind him,
and very soon found
an opportunity of taking it away.
She did it so quickly
that the poor little juror
(it was Bill, the Lizard)
could not make out at all
what had become of it; so,
after hunting all about for it,

he was obliged to write
with one finger
for the rest of the day;
and this was of very little use,
as it left no mark on the slate.

"Herald, read the accusation!"
said the King.

On this the White Rabbit blew
three blasts on the trumpet,
and then unrolled
the parchment scroll,
and read as follows:—

"The Queen of Hearts,
she made some tarts,
        All on a summer day:
The Knave of Hearts,
he stole those tarts,
        And took them quite away!"

"Consider your verdict,"
the King said to the jury.

"Not yet, not yet!"
the Rabbit hastily interrupted.
"There's a great deal
to come before that!"

"Call the first witness,"
said the King;
and the White Rabbit
blew three blasts on the trumpet,
and called out, "First witness!"

The first witness was the Hatter.
He came in with a teacup
in one hand and a piece
of bread-and-butter in the other.
"I beg pardon, your Majesty,"
he began, "for bringing these in:
but I hadn't quite finished my tea
when I was sent for."

"You ought to have finished,"
said the King.
"When did you begin?"

The Hatter
looked at the March Hare,
who had followed him
into the court,
arm-in-arm with the Dormouse.
"Fourteenth of March,
I think it was," he said.

"Fifteenth," said the March Hare.

"Sixteenth,"
added the Dormouse.

"Write that down,"
the King said to the jury,
and the jury eagerly wrote down
all three dates on their slates,
and then added them up,
and reduced the answer
to shillings and pence.

"Take off your hat,"
the King said to the Hatter.

"It isn't mine," said the Hatter.

"Stolen!" the King exclaimed,
turning to the jury,
who instantly
made a memorandum of the fact.

"I keep them to sell,"
the Hatter added
as an explanation;
"I've none of my own.
I'm a hatter."

Here the Queen
put on her spectacles,

and began staring at the Hatter,
who turned pale and fidgeted.

"Give your evidence,"
said the King;"
and don't be nervous,
or I'll have you
executed on the spot."

This did not seem
to encourage the witness at all:
he kept shifting from one foot
to the other,
looking uneasily at the Queen,
and in his confusion he bit
a large piece out of his teacup
instead of the bread-and-butter.

Just at this moment Alice
felt a very curious sensation,
which puzzled her a good deal
until she made out what it was:
she was beginning
to grow larger again,
and she thought at first
she would get up
and leave the court;
but on second thoughts
she decided to remain
where she was as long
as there was room for her.
"I wish you
wouldn't squeeze so."
said the Dormouse,
who was sitting next to her.
"I can hardly breathe."

"I can't help it,"
said Alice very meekly:
"I'm growing."

"You've no right to grow here,"
said the Dormouse.

"Don't talk nonsense,"
said Alice more boldly:
"you know you're growing too."

"Yes,
but I grow at a reasonable pace,"
said the Dormouse:
"not in that ridiculous fashion."
And he got up very sulkily
and crossed over
to the other side of the court.

All this time the Queen
had never left off staring
at the Hatter, and,
just as the Dormouse
crossed the court,
she said to one
of the officers of the court,
"Bring me the list of the singers
in the last concert!" on which
the wretched Hatter trembled so,
that he shook both his shoes off.

"Give your evidence,"
the King repeated angrily,
"or I'll have you executed,
whether you're nervous or not."

"I'm a poor man, your Majesty,"
the Hatter began,
in a trembling voice,
"—and I hadn't
begun my tea—
not above a week or so—
and what with the bread-
and-butter getting so thin—
and the twinkling of the tea—"

"The twinkling of the what?"
said the King.

"It began with the tea,"
the Hatter replied.

"Of course twinkling begins
with a T!" said the King sharply.
"Do you take me for a dunce?
Go on!"

"I'm a poor man,"
the Hatter went on,
"and most things
twinkled after that—
only the March Hare said—"

"I didn't!" the March Hare
interrupted in a great hurry.

"You did!" said the Hatter.

"I deny it!" said the March Hare.

"He denies it," said the King:
"leave out that part."

"Well, at any rate,
the Dormouse said—"
the Hatter went on,
looking anxiously round
to see if he would deny it too:
but the Dormouse
denied nothing,
being fast asleep.

"After that," continued the Hatter,
"I cut some more bread-
and-butter—"

"But what did
the Dormouse say?"
one of the jury asked.

"That I can't remember,"
said the Hatter.

"You must remember,"
remarked the King,

"or I'll have you executed."

The miserable Hatter
dropped his teacup
and bread-and-butter,
and went down on one knee.
"I'm a poor man,
your Majesty," he began.

"You're a very poor speaker,"
said the King.

Here one
of the guinea-pigs cheered,
and was immediately suppressed
by the officers of the court.

(As that is rather a hard word,
I will just explain to you
how it was done.
They had a large canvas bag,
which tied up at the mouth
with strings:
into this they slipped
the guinea-pig,
head first, and then sat upon it.)

"I'm glad I've seen that done,"
thought Alice.
"I've so often read
in the newspapers,
at the end of trials,
"There was some attempts
at applause,
which was
immediately suppressed
by the officers of the court,
"and I never understood
what it meant till now."

"If that's all you know about it,
you may stand down,"
continued the King.

"I can't go no lower,"
said the Hatter:
"I'm on the floor, as it is."

"Then you may sit down,"
the King replied.

Here the other guinea-pig
cheered, and was suppressed.

"Come,
that finished the guinea-pigs!"
thought Alice.
"Now we shall get on better."

"I'd rather finish my tea,"
said the Hatter,
with an anxious look
at the Queen,
who was reading
the list of singers.

"You may go," said the King,
and the Hatter hurriedly
left the court,
without even waiting
to put his shoes on.

"—and just take his head off
outside," the Queen added
to one of the officers:
but the Hatter was out of sight
before the officer
could get to the door.

"Call the next witness!"
said the King.

The next witness
was the Duchess's cook.
She carried the pepper-box
in her hand,
and Alice guessed who it was,
even before she got into the court,

by the way the people
near the door
began sneezing all at once.

"Give your evidence,"
 said the King.

"Shan't," said the cook.

The King looked anxiously
at the White Rabbit,
who said in a low voice,
"Your Majesty
must cross-examine
this witness."

"Well, if I must, I must,"
the King said,
with a melancholy air,
and, after folding his arms
and frowning at the cook
till his eyes
were nearly out of sight,
he said in a deep voice,
"What are tarts made of?"

"Pepper, mostly," said the cook.

"Treacle,"
said a sleepy voice behind her.

"Collar that Dormouse,"
the Queen shrieked out.
"Behead that Dormouse!
Turn that Dormouse out of court!
Suppress him! Pinch him!
Off with his whiskers!"

For some minutes
the whole court was in confusion,
getting the Dormouse turned out,
and, by the time
they had settled down again,
the cook had disappeared.

"Never mind!" said the King,
with an air of great relief.
"Call the next witness."
And he added
in an undertone to the Queen,
"Really, my dear,
you must cross-examine
the next witness.
It quite makes
my forehead ache!"

Alice watched the White Rabbit
as he fumbled over the list,
feeling very curious to see
what the next witness
would be like,
"—for they haven't got much
evidence yet ," she said to herself.
Imagine her surprise,
when the White Rabbit read out,
at the top of his shrill little voice,
the name "Alice!"

CHAPTER XII.

Alice's Evidence

"Here!" cried Alice,
quite forgetting
in the flurry of the moment
how large she had grown
in the last few minutes,
and she jumped up
in such a hurry
that she tipped over the jury-box
with the edge of her skirt,
upsetting all the jurymen
on to the heads
of the crowd below,
and there they lay
sprawling about,
reminding her very much
of a globe of goldfish
she had accidentally upset
the week before.

"Oh, I beg your pardon!"
she exclaimed
in a tone of great dismay,
and began picking them up again
as quickly as she could,
for the accident of the goldfish
kept running in her head,
and she had a vague sort of idea
that they must be
collected at once
and put back into the jury-box,
or they would die.

"The trial cannot proceed,"
said the King
in a very grave voice,
"until all the jurymen are back
in their proper places— all,"
he repeated with great emphasis,
looking hard at Alice
as he said so.

Alice looked at the jury-box,
and saw that, in her haste,
she had put the Lizard
in head downwards,
and the poor little thing
was waving its tail
about in a melancholy way,
being quite unable to move.
She soon got it out again,
and put it right;
"not that it signifies much,"
she said to herself;
"I should think it would be
quite as much use in the trial
one way up as the other."

As soon as the jury
had a little recovered
from the shock of being upset,
and their slates and pencils
had been found
and handed back to them,
they set to work very diligently
to write out a history
of the accident,
all except the Lizard,
who seemed too much overcome
to do anything but sit
with its mouth open,
gazing up into the roof
of the court.

"What do you know
about this business?"
the King said to Alice.

"Nothing," said Alice.

"Nothing whatever?"
persisted the King.

"Nothing whatever," said Alice.

"That's very important,"
the King said, turning to the jury.
They were just beginning
to write this down on their slates,
when the White Rabbit
interrupted: "Un important,
your Majesty means, of course,"
he said in a very respectful tone,
but frowning and making faces
at him as he spoke.

"Un important,
of course, I meant,"
the King hastily said,
and went on to himself
in an undertone,

"important—unimportant—
unimportant—important—"
 as if he were trying
which word sounded best.

Some of the jury wrote it down
"important,"
and some "unimportant."
Alice could see this,
as she was near enough
to look over their slates;
"but it doesn't matter a bit,"
she thought to herself.

At this moment the King,
who had been for some time
busily writing in his note-book,
cackled out "Silence!"
and read out from his book,
"Rule Forty-two.
All persons more than a mile high
to leave the court .
"

Everybody looked at Alice.

"I'm not a mile high," said Alice.

"You are," said the King.

"Nearly two miles high,"
added the Queen.

"Well, I shan't go,
at any rate," said Alice:
"besides, that's not a regular rule:
you invented it just now."

"It's the oldest rule in the book,"
said the King.

"Then it ought to be
Number One," said Alice.

The King turned pale,
and shut his note-book hastily.
"Consider your verdict,"
he said to the jury,
in a low, trembling voice.

"There's more evidence
to come yet,
please your Majesty,"
said the White Rabbit,
jumping up in a great hurry;
"this paper
has just been picked up."

"What's in it?" said the Queen.

"I haven't opened it yet,"
said the White Rabbit,
"but it seems to be a letter,
written by the prisoner to—
to somebody."

"It must have been that,"
said the King,
"unless it was written to nobody,
which isn't usual, you know."

"Who is it directed to?"
said one of the jurymen.

"It isn't directed at all,"
said the White Rabbit; "in fact,
there's nothing written
on the outside."
He unfolded the paper
as he spoke, and added
"It isn't a letter, after all:
it's a set of verses."

"Are they in
the prisoner's handwriting?"
asked another of the jurymen.

"No, they're not,"
said the White Rabbit,
"and that's the queerest thing
about it."
(The jury all looked puzzled.)

"He must have imitated
somebody else's hand,"
said the King.

(The jury
all brightened up again.)

"Please your Majesty,"
said the Knave,
"I didn't write it,
and they can't prove I did:
there's no name signed
at the end."

"If you didn't sign it,"
said the King,
"that only makes
the matter worse.
You must have meant
some mischief,
or else you'd have signed
your name like an honest man."

There was a general
clapping of hands at this:
it was the first really clever thing
the King had said that day.

"That proves his guilt,"
said the Queen.

"It proves nothing of the sort!"
said Alice. "Why,
you don't even know
what they're about!"

"Read them," said the King.

The White Rabbit
put on his spectacles.
"Where shall I begin,
please your Majesty?" he asked.

"Begin at the beginning,"
the King said gravely,
"and go on till you come
to the end: then stop."

These were the verses
the White Rabbit read:—

"They told me
you had been to her,
    And mentioned me to him:
She gave me a good character,
    But said I could not swim.
He sent them word
I had not gone
 (We know it to be true):
If she should push the matter on,
    What would become of you?

I gave her one,
they gave him two,
 You gave us three or more;
They all returned

from him to you,
    Though they were mine before.

If I or she should chance to be
        Involved in this affair,
He trusts to you to set them free,
        Exactly as we were.
My notion was that you had been
        (Before she had this fit)
An obstacle that came between
        Him, and ourselves, and it.

Don't let him know
she liked them best,
        For this must ever be
A secret, kept from all the rest,
        Between yourself and me."

"That's the most important
piece of evidence
we've heard yet,"
said the King, rubbing his hands;
"so now let the jury—"

"If any one of them
can explain it," said Alice,

(she had grown so large
in the last few minutes
that she wasn't a bit afraid
of interrupting him,)
"I'll give him sixpence.
I don't believe
there's an atom of meaning in it."

The jury all wrote down
on their slates,
"She doesn't believe
there's an atom of meaning in it,"
but none of them attempted
to explain the paper.

"If there's no meaning in it,"
said the King,

"that saves a world of trouble,
you know,
as we needn't try to find any.
And yet I don't know,"
he went on,
spreading out the verses
on his knee,
and looking at them with one eye;
"I seem to see some meaning
in them, after all.
" — said I could not swim —"
 you can't swim, can you?"
he added,
turning to the Knave.

The Knave shook his head sadly.
"Do I look like it?" he said.

(Which he certainly did not ,
being made entirely
of cardboard.)

"All right, so far," said the King,
and he went on muttering over
the verses to himself:" '
We know it to be true —'
that's the jury, of course—
 ' I gave her one,
they gave him two —' why,
that must be what he did
with the tarts, you know—"

"But, it goes on' they all returned
from him to you,' " said Alice.

"Why, there they are!"
said the King triumphantly,
pointing to the tarts on the table.
"Nothing can be clearer
than that. Then again—
 ' before she had this fit —'
you never had fits, my dear,
I think?" he said to the Queen.

"Never!"
said the Queen furiously,
throwing an inkstand
at the Lizard as she spoke.

(The unfortunate little Bill
had left off writing on his slate
with one finger,
as he found it made no mark;
but he now hastily began again,
using the ink,
that was trickling down his face,
as long as it lasted.)

"Then the words don't fit you,"
said the King,
looking round the court
with a smile.
There was a dead silence.

"It's a pun!" the King added
in an offended tone,
and everybody laughed,
"Let the jury
consider their verdict,"
the King said,
for about the twentieth time
that day.

"No, no!" said the Queen.
"Sentence first —
verdict afterwards."

"Stuff and nonsense!"
said Alice loudly. "The idea
of having the sentence first!"

"Hold your tongue!"
said the Queen, turning purple.

"I won't!" said Alice.

"Off with her head!"
the Queen shouted
at the top of her voice.
Nobody moved.

"Who cares for you?" said Alice,

(she had grown to her full size
by this time.)
"You're nothing
but a pack of cards!"

At this the whole pack
rose up into the air,
and came flying down upon her:
she gave a little scream,
half of fright and half of anger,
and tried to beat them off,
and found herself lying
on the bank, with her head
in the lap of her sister,
who was gently brushing away
some dead leaves
that had fluttered down
from the trees upon her face.

"Wake up, Alice dear!"
said her sister; "Why,
what a long sleep you've had!"

"Oh,
I've had such a curious dream!"
said Alice, and she told her sister,
as well as she could
remember them, all these strange
Adventures of hers that you have
just been reading about;
and when she had finished,
her sister kissed her, and said,
"It was a curious dream,
dear, certainly:
but now run in to your tea;
it's getting late."
So Alice got up and ran off,
thinking while she ran,
as well she might,

what a wonderful dream
it had been.

But her sister sat still
just as she left her,
leaning her head on her hand,
watching the setting sun,
and thinking of little Alice
and all her
wonderful Adventures,
till she too began dreaming
after a fashion,
and this was her dream:—

First,
she dreamed of little Alice herself,
and once again the tiny hands
were clasped upon her knee,
and the bright eager eyes
were looking up into hers—
she could hear the very tones
of her voice,
and see that queer little toss
of her head to keep back
the wandering hair
that would always
get into her eyes—
and still as she listened,
or seemed to listen,
the whole place around her
became alive
with the strange creatures
of her little sister's dream.

The long grass rustled at her feet
as the White Rabbit hurried by—
the frightened Mouse
splashed his way through
the neighbouring pool—
she could hear the rattle
of the teacups as the March Hare
and his friends
shared their never-ending meal,
and the shrill voice of the Queen

ordering off
her unfortunate guests
to execution—
once more the pig-baby
was sneezing
on the Duchess's knee,
while plates and dishes
crashed around it—
once more the shriek
of the Gryphon,
the squeaking
of the Lizard's slate-pencil,
and the choking
of the suppressed guinea-pigs,
filled the air,
mixed up with the distant sobs
of the miserable Mock Turtle.

So she sat on, with closed eyes,
and half believed herself
in Wonderland,
though she knew she had
but to open them again,
and all would change
to dull reality—
the grass would be only
rustling in the wind,
and the pool rippling
to the waving of the reeds—
the rattling teacups would change
to tinkling sheep-bells,
and the Queen's shrill cries
to the voice
of the shepherd boy—
and the sneeze of the baby,
the shriek of the Gryphon,
and all the other queer noises,
would change (she knew)
to the confused clamour
of the busy farm-yard—
while the lowing of the cattle
in the distance
would take the place
of the Mock Turtle's heavy sobs.

Lastly,
she pictured to herself
how this same little sister
of hers would, in the after-time,
be herself a grown woman;
and how she would keep,
through all her riper years,
the simple and loving heart
of her childhood:
and how she would gather
about her other little children,
and make their eyes bright and
eager with many a strange tale,
perhaps even with the dream
of Wonderland of long ago:
and how she would feel
with all their simple sorrows,
and find a pleasure
in all their simple joys,
remembering her own child-life,
and the happy summer days.

THE END

Through The Looking-Glass And What Alice Found There

By Lewis Carroll: Stacked Prose Edition

TABLE OF CONTENTS

CHAPTER I.   Looking-Glass house.............................. 83
CHAPTER II.   The Garden of Live Flowers..................... 92
CHAPTER III.   Looking-Glass Insects........................... 100
CHAPTER IV.   Tweedledum And Tweedledee 109
CHAPTER V.   Wool and Water 119
CHAPTER VI.   Humpty Dumpty 128
CHAPTER VII.   The Lion and the Unicorn...................... 138
CHAPTER VIII.   "It's my own Invention" 146
CHAPTER IX.   Queen Alice 158
CHAPTER X.   Shaking... 170
CHAPTER XI.   Waking 170
CHAPTER XII.   Which Dreamed it? 170

CHAPTER I.

Looking-Glass house

One thing was certain,
that the white kitten had had
nothing to do with it:
—it was the black kitten's
fault entirely.
For the white kitten
had been having its face washed
by the old cat
for the last quarter of an hour
(and bearing it pretty well,
considering);
so you see that it couldn't have
had any hand in the mischief.

The way Dinah
washed her children's faces
was this: first she held
the poor thing down
by its ear with one paw,
and then with the other paw
she rubbed its face all over,
the wrong way,
beginning at the nose:
and just now, as I said,
she was hard at work
on the white kitten,
which was lying quite still
and trying to purr—
no doubt feeling
that it was all meant for its good.

But the black kitten
had been finished with earlier
in the afternoon, and so,
while Alice was sitting
curled up in a corner
of the great arm-chair,
half talking to herself
and half asleep,
the kitten had been

having a grand game of romps
with the ball of worsted
Alice had been trying to wind up,
and had been rolling it up
and down till
it had all come undone again;
and there it was,
spread over the hearth-rug,
all knots and tangles,
with the kitten running
after its own tail in the middle.

"Oh, you wicked little thing!"
cried Alice, catching up the kitten,
and giving it a little kiss
to make it understand
that it was in disgrace.
"Really, Dinah ought to have
taught you better manners!
You ought, Dinah,
you know you ought!"
she added, looking reproachfully
at the old cat,
and speaking in as cross
a voice as she could manage—
and then she scrambled back
into the arm-chair,
taking the kitten
and the worsted with her,
and began winding up
the ball again.
But she didn't get on very fast,
as she was talking all the time,
sometimes to the kitten,
and sometimes to herself.
Kitty sat very demurely
on her knee, pretending to watch
the progress of the winding,
and now and then putting out
one paw and gently
touching the ball,
as if it would be glad to help,
if it might.

"Do you know
what to-morrow is, Kitty?"
Alice began.
"You'd have guessed
if you'd been up
in the window with me—
only Dinah was making you tidy,
so you couldn't.
I was watching the boys
getting in sticks for the bonfire—
and it wants plenty of sticks,
Kitty! Only it got so cold,
and it snowed so,
they had to leave off.
Never mind, Kitty, we'll go
and see the bonfire to-morrow."
Here Alice wound
two or three turns of the worsted
round the kitten's neck,
just to see how it would look:
this led to a scramble,
in which the ball
rolled down upon the floor,
and yards and yards of it
got unwound again.

"Do you know,
I was so angry, Kitty,"
Alice went on as soon as they
were comfortably settled again,
"when I saw all the mischief
you had been doing,
I was very nearly
opening the window,
and putting you out
into the snow!
And you'd have deserved it,
you little mischievous darling!
What have you got to say
for yourself?
Now don't interrupt me!"
she went on,
holding up one finger.
"I'm going to tell you

all your faults. Number one:
you squeaked twice while Dinah
was washing your face
this morning.
Now you can't deny it, Kitty:
I heard you!
What's that you say?"
(pretending that the kitten
was speaking.)
"Her paw went into your eye?
Well, that's your fault,
for keeping your eyes open—
if you'd shut them tight up,
it wouldn't have happened.
Now don't make
any more excuses, but listen!
Number two:
you pulled Snowdrop away
by the tail just as I had
put down the saucer of milk
before her! What,
you were thirsty, were you?
How do you know
she wasn't thirsty too?
Now for number three:
you unwound every bit
of the worsted
while I wasn't looking!

"That's three faults, Kitty,
and you've not been punished
for any of them yet.
You know I'm saving up
all your punishments
for Wednesday week—
Suppose they had saved up
all my punishments!"
she went on,
talking more to herself
than the kitten.
"What would they do
at the end of a year?
I should be sent to prison,
I suppose, when the day came.

Or—let me see—
suppose each punishment
was to be going without a dinner:
then,
when the miserable day came,
I should have to go without
fifty dinners at once! Well,
I shouldn't mind that much!
I'd far rather go without them
than eat them!

"Do you hear the snow
against the window-panes,
Kitty?
How nice and soft it sounds!
Just as if some one was kissing
the window all over outside.
I wonder if the snow
loves the trees and fields,
that it kisses them so gently?
And then it covers them up snug,
you know, with a white quilt;
and perhaps it says,
'Go to sleep, darlings,
till the summer comes again.'
And when they wake up
in the summer, Kitty,
they dress themselves
all in green, and dance about—
whenever the wind blows—oh,
that's very pretty!" cried Alice,
dropping the ball
of worsted to clap her hands.
"And I do so wish it was true!
I'm sure the woods look sleepy
in the autumn,
when the leaves
are getting brown.

"Kitty, can you play chess? Now,
don't smile, my dear,
I'm asking it seriously.
Because,
when we were playing just now,

you watched
just as if you understood it:
and when I said 'Check!'
you purred!
Well, it was a nice check, Kitty,
and really I might have won,
if it hadn't been
for that nasty Knight,
that came wiggling down
among my pieces. Kitty, dear,
let's pretend—" And here I wish
I could tell you half the things
Alice used to say, beginning
with her favourite phrase
"Let's pretend." She had had
quite a long argument
with her sister
only the day before—
all because Alice
had begun with "Let's pretend
we're kings and queens;"
and her sister,
who liked being very exact,
had argued that they couldn't,
because
there were only two of them,
and Alice
had been reduced at last to say,
"Well,
you can be one of them then,
and I'll be all the rest."
And once she had really
frightened her old nurse
by shouting suddenly in her ear,
"Nurse! Do let's pretend
that I'm a hungry hyaena,
and you're a bone."

But this is taking us away
from Alice's speech to the kitten.
"Let's pretend that
you're the Red Queen,
Kitty! Do you know,
I think if you sat up

and folded your arms,
you'd look exactly like her.
Now do try, there's a dear!"
And Alice
got the Red Queen off the table,
and set it up before the kitten
as a model for it to imitate:
however,
the thing didn't succeed,
principally, Alice said,
because the kitten
wouldn't fold its arms properly.
So, to punish it, she held it up
to the Looking-glass,
that it might see
how sulky it was—
"and if you're not good directly,"
she added,
"I'll put you through
into Looking-glass House.
How would you like that?"

"Now,
if you'll only attend, Kitty,
and not talk so much,
I'll tell you all my ideas
about Looking-glass House.
First, there's the room
you can see through the glass —
that's just the same
as our drawing room,
only the things go the other way.
I can see all of it
when I get upon a chair—
all but the bit
behind the fireplace. Oh!
I do so wish I could see that bit!
I want so much to know whether
they've a fire in the winter:
you never can tell, you know,
unless our fire smokes,
and then smoke comes up
in that room too—
but that may be only pretence,

just to make it look
as if they had a fire. Well then,
the books are something
like our books, only the words
go the wrong way; I know that,
because I've held up
one of our books to the glass,
and then they hold up one
in the other room.

"How would you like
to live in Looking-glass House,
Kitty?
I wonder if they'd
give you milk in there?
Perhaps Looking-glass milk
isn't good to drink—But oh,
Kitty!
now we come to the passage.
You can just see
a little peep of the passage
in Looking-glass House,
if you leave the door
of our drawing-room wide open:
and it's very like our passage
as far as you can see,
only you know it may be
quite different on beyond.
Oh, Kitty!
how nice it would be
if we could only get through
into Looking-glass House!
I'm sure it's got, oh!
such beautiful things in it!
Let's pretend there's a way
of getting through into it,
somehow, Kitty.
Let's pretend the glass
has got all soft like gauze,
so that we can get through.
Why, it's turning
into a sort of mist now, I declare!
It'll be easy enough
to get through—"

She was up on the chimney-piece
while she said this,
though she hardly knew
how she had got there.
And certainly the glass
was beginning to melt away,
just like a bright silvery mist.

In another moment Alice
was through the glass,
and had jumped lightly down
into the Looking-glass room.
The very first thing she did
was to look whether
there was a fire in the fireplace,
and she was quite pleased to find
that there was a real one,
blazing away as brightly
as the one she had left behind.
"So I shall be as warm here
as I was in the old room,"
thought Alice: "warmer, in fact,
because there'll be no one here to
scold me away from the fire. Oh,
what fun it'll be,
when they see me
through the glass in here,
and can't get at me!"

Then she began looking about,
and noticed that
what could be seen
from the old room
was quite common
and uninteresting,
but that all the rest
was as different as possible.
For instance,
the pictures on the wall
next the fire
seemed to be all alive,
and the very clock
on the chimney-piece
(you know you can only see the

back of it in the Looking-glass)
had got the face
of a little old man,
and grinned at her.

"They don't keep this room
so tidy as the other,"
Alice thought to herself,
as she noticed
several of the chessmen
down in the hearth
among the cinders:
but in another moment,
with a little "Oh!" of surprise,
she was down on her hands
and knees watching them.
The chessmen
were walking about,
two and two!

"Here are the Red King
and the Red Queen," Alice said
(in a whisper,
for fear of frightening them),
"and there are the White King
and the White Queen
sitting on the edge of the shovel—
and here are two castles
walking arm in arm—
I don't think they can hear me,"
she went on,
as she put her head closer down,
"and I'm nearly sure
they can't see me.
I feel somehow
as if I were invisible—"

Here something began squeaking
on the table behind Alice,
and made her turn her head
just in time to see
one of the White Pawns
roll over and begin kicking:
she watched it

with great curiosity
to see what would happen next.

"It is the voice of my child!"
the White Queen cried out
as she rushed past the King,
so violently that she knocked him
over among the cinders.
"My precious Lily!
My imperial kitten!"
and she began scrambling
wildly up the side of the fender.

"Imperial fiddlestick!"
said the King, rubbing his nose,
which had been hurt by the fall.
He had a right to be
a little annoyed with the Queen,
for he was covered
with ashes from head to foot.

Alice was very anxious to be
of use, and, as the poor little Lily
was nearly
screaming herself into a fit,
she hastily picked up the Queen
and set her on the table
by the side
of her noisy little daughter.

The Queen gasped,
and sat down:
the rapid journey through the air
had quite taken away her breath
and for a minute or two
she could do nothing
but hug the little Lily in silence.
As soon as she had recovered
her breath a little,
she called out to the White King,
who was sitting sulkily
among the ashes,
"Mind the volcano!"

"What volcano?" said the King,
looking up anxiously into the fire,
as if he thought that was
the most likely place to find one.

"Blew—me—up,"
panted the Queen,
who was still a little out of breath.
"Mind you come up—
the regular way—
don't get blown up!"

Alice watched the White King
as he slowly struggled up
from bar to bar,
till at last she said, "Why,
you'll be hours and hours
getting to the table, at that rate.
I'd far better help you, hadn't I?"
But the King
took no notice of the question:
it was quite clear that he
could neither hear her
nor see her.

So Alice picked him up
very gently,
and lifted him across more slowly
than she had lifted the Queen,
that she mightn't
take his breath away: but,
before she put him on the table,
she thought she might as well
dust him a little,
he was so covered with ashes.

She said afterwards that she had
never seen in all her life
such a face as the King made,
when he found himself
held in the air
by an invisible hand,
and being dusted:
he was far too much astonished

to cry out,
but his eyes and his mouth
went on getting larger and larger,
and rounder and rounder,
till her hand shook
so with laughing that she nearly
let him drop upon the floor.

"Oh!
please don't make such faces,
my dear!" she cried out,
quite forgetting
that the King couldn't hear her.
"You make me laugh
so that I can hardly hold you!
And don't keep your mouth
so wide open!
All the ashes will get into it—
there,
now I think you're tidy enough!"
she added,
as she smoothed his hair,
and set him upon the table
near the Queen.

The King
immediately fell flat on his back,
and lay perfectly still:
and Alice was a little alarmed
at what she had done,
and went round the room
to see if she could find any water
to throw over him. However,
she could find nothing
but a bottle of ink,
and when she got back with it
she found he had recovered,
and he and the Queen
were talking together
in a frightened whisper—so low,
that Alice could hardly hear
what they said.

The King was saying,

"I assure, you my dear,
I turned cold
to the very ends of my whiskers!"

To which the Queen replied,
"You haven't got any whiskers."

"The horror of that moment,"
the King went on,
"I shall never, never forget!"

"You will, though,"
the Queen said, "if you don't
make a memorandum of it."

Alice looked on
with great interest
as the King took an enormous
memorandum-book
out of his pocket,
and began writing.
A sudden thought struck her,
and she took hold
of the end of the pencil,
which came some way
over his shoulder,
and began writing for him.

The poor King
looked puzzled and unhappy,
and struggled with the pencil
for some time
without saying anything;
but Alice was too strong for him,
and at last he panted out,
"My dear!
I really must get a thinner pencil.
I can't manage this one a bit;
it writes all manner of things
that I don't intend—"

"What manner of things?"
said the Queen,
looking over the book

(in which Alice had put
"The White Knight
is sliding down the poker.
He balances very badly")
"That's not a memorandum
of your feelings!"

There was a book
lying near Alice on the table,
and while she sat
watching the White King
(for she was still
a little anxious about him,
and had the ink
all ready to throw over him,
in case he fainted again),
she turned over the leaves,
to find some part
that she could read,
"—for it's all in some language
I don't know," she said to herself.

It was like this.

.YKCOWREBBAJ

sevot yhtils eht dna, gillirb sawT'
ebaw eht ni elbmig dna eryg diD
  ,sevogorob eht erew ysmim llA
.ebargtuo shtar emom eht dnA

She puzzled over this
for some time,
but at last a bright thought
struck her.
"Why, it's a Looking-glass book,
of course!
And if I hold it up to a glass,
the words will all go
the right way again."

This was the poem
that Alice read.

JABBERWOCKY.

'Twas brillig, and the slithy toves
  Did gyre and gimble in the wabe;
All mimsy were the borogoves,
  And the mome raths outgrabe.

"Beware the Jabberwock, my son!
  The jaws that bite,
  the claws that catch!
Beware the Jubjub bird, and shun
  The frumious Bandersnatch!"

He took his vorpal sword
     in hand:
Long time the manxome foe
     he sought—
So rested he by the Tumtum tree,
  And stood awhile in thought.

And as in uffish thought
     he stood,
The Jabberwock,
     with eyes of flame,
Came whiffling
     through the tulgey wood,
And burbled as it came!

One, two! One, two!
And through and through
  The vorpal blade
     went snicker-snack!
He left it dead, and with its head
  He went galumphing back.

"And hast thou
     slain the Jabberwock?
Come to my arms,
     my beamish boy!
O frabjous day!
     Callooh! Callay!"
He chortled in his joy.

'Twas brillig,

and the slithy toves
Did gyre and gimble
in the wabe;
All mimsy were the borogoves,
 And the mome raths outgrabe.

"It seems very pretty," she said
when she had finished it,
"but it's rather
hard to understand!"
(You see she didn't
like to confess, even to herself,
that she couldn't
make it out at all.)
"Somehow it seems to fill
my head with ideas—
only I don't exactly know
what they are! However,
somebody killed something :
that's clear, at any rate—"

"But oh!" thought Alice,
suddenly jumping up,
"if I don't make haste I shall have
to go back through
the Looking-glass,
before I've seen what the rest
of the house is like!
Let's have a look
at the garden first!"
She was out of the room
in a moment,
and ran down stairs—or, at least,
it wasn't exactly running,
but a new invention of hers
for getting down stairs
quickly and easily,
as Alice said to herself.
She just kept the tips
of her fingers on the hand-rail,
and floated gently down
without even touching the stairs
with her feet;
then she floated on

through the hall,
and would have gone straight out
at the door in the same way,
if she hadn't caught hold
of the door-post.
She was getting a little giddy
with so much floating in the air,
and was rather glad to find
herself walking again
in the natural way.

CHAPTER II.

The Garden of Live Flowers

"I should see the garden
far better," said Alice to herself,
"if I could get
to the top of that hill:
and here's a path
that leads straight to it—at least,
no, it doesn't do that—"
(after going a few yards
along the path, and turning
several sharp corners),
"but I suppose it will at last.
But how curiously it twists!
It's more like a corkscrew
than a path! Well,
this turn goes to the hill,
I suppose—no, it doesn't!
This goes straight back
to the house! Well then,
I'll try it the other way."

And so she did:
wandering up and down,
and trying turn after turn,
but always coming back
to the house, do what she would.
Indeed, once,
when she turned a corner
rather more quickly than usual,
she ran against it
before she could stop herself.

"It's no use talking about it,"
Alice said,
looking up at the house
and pretending it
was arguing with her.
"I'm not going in again yet.
I know I should have
to get through
the Looking-glass again—

back into the old room—
and there'd be an end
of all my adventures!"

So, resolutely turning her back
upon the house, she set out
once more down the path,
determined to keep straight
on till she got to the hill.
For a few minutes
all went on well,
and she was just saying,
"I really shall do it this time—"
when the path
gave a sudden twist
and shook itself
(as she described it afterwards),
and the next moment
she found herself
actually walking in at the door.

"Oh, it's too bad!" she cried.
"I never saw such a house
for getting in the way! Never!"

However,
there was the hill full in sight,
so there was nothing to be done
but start again.
This time she came upon
a large flower-bed,
with a border of daisies,
and a willow-tree growing
in the middle.

"O Tiger-lily," said Alice,
addressing herself to one
that was waving gracefully
about in the wind,
"I wish you could talk!"

"We can talk," said the Tiger-lily:
"when there's anybody
worth talking to."

Alice was so astonished
that she could not speak
for a minute: it quite seemed
to take her breath away.
At length, as the Tiger-lily
only went on waving about,
she spoke again,
in a timid voice—
almost in a whisper.
"And can all the flowers talk?"

"As well as you can,"
said the Tiger-lily.
"And a great deal louder."

"It isn't manners for us to begin,
you know," said the Rose,
"and I really was wondering
when you'd speak!
Said I to myself,
'Her face has got some sense in it,
though it's not a clever one!' Still,
you're the right colour,
and that goes a long way."

"I don't care about the colour,"
the Tiger-lily remarked.
"If only her petals curled up
a little more, she'd be all right."

Alice didn't like being criticised,
so she began asking questions.
"Aren't you sometimes frightened
at being planted out here,
with nobody to take care of you?"

"There's the tree in the middle,"
said the Rose:
"what else is it good for?"

"But what could it do,
if any danger came?" Alice asked.

"It says 'Bough-wough!' "
cried a Daisy:
"that's why its branches
are called boughs!"

"Didn't you know that?"
cried another Daisy,
and here they all began
shouting together, till the air
seemed quite full
of little shrill voices.
"Silence, every one of you!"
cried the Tiger-lily,
waving itself passionately
from side to side,
and trembling with excitement.
"They know I can't get at them!"
it panted,
bending its quivering head
towards Alice,
"or they wouldn't dare to do it!"

"Never mind!"
Alice said in a soothing tone,
and stooping down to the daisies,
who were just beginning again,
she whispered,
"If you don't hold your tongues,
I'll pick you!"

There was silence in a moment,
and several of the pink daisies
turned white.

"That's right!" said the Tiger-lily.
"The daisies are worst of all.
When one speaks,
they all begin together,
and it's enough
to make one wither
to hear the way they go on!"

"How is it you can all talk
so nicely?" Alice said,

hoping to get it into
a better temper by a compliment.
"I've been in
many gardens before, but none
of the flowers could talk."

"Put your hand down,
and feel the ground,"
said the Tiger-lily.
"Then you'll know why."

Alice did so. "It's very hard,"
she said, "but I don't see
what that has to do with it."

"In most gardens,"
the Tiger-lily said,
"they make the beds too soft—
so that the flowers
are always asleep."

This sounded a very good reason,
and Alice was quite pleased
to know it.
"I never thought of that before!"
she said.

"It's my opinion
that you never think at all,"
the Rose said
in a rather severe tone.

"I never saw anybody
that looked stupider,"
a Violet said, so suddenly,
that Alice quite jumped;
for it hadn't spoken before.

"Hold your tongue!"
cried the Tiger-lily.
"As if you ever saw anybody!
You keep your head
under the leaves,
and snore away there,

till you know no more
what's going on in the world,
than if you were a bud!"

"Are there any more people
in the garden besides me?"
Alice said, not choosing to notice
the Rose's last remark.

"There's one other flower
in the garden
that can move about like you,"
said the Rose.
"I wonder how you do it—"
("You're always wondering,"
said the Tiger-lily),
"but she's more bushy
than you are."

"Is she like me?"
Alice asked eagerly,
for the thought crossed her mind,
"There's another little girl
in the garden, somewhere!"

"Well,
she has the same awkward shape
as you," the Rose said,
"but she's redder— and
her petals are shorter, I think."

"Her petals are done up close,
almost like a dahlia,"
the Tiger-lily interrupted:
"not tumbled about anyhow,
like yours."

"But that's not your fault,"
the Rose added kindly:
"you're beginning to fade,
you know— and then one
can't help one's petals
getting a little untidy."

Alice didn't like this idea at all:
so, to change the subject,
she asked
"Does she ever come out here?"

"I daresay you'll see her soon,"
said the Rose.
"She's one of the thorny kind."

"Where does
she wear the horns?"
Alice asked with some curiosity.

"Why all round her head,
of course," the Rose replied.
"I was wondering
you hadn't got some too.
I thought it was the regular rule."

"She's coming!"
cried the Larkspur.
"I hear her footstep,
thump, thump, thump,
along the gravel-walk!"

Alice looked round eagerly,
and found that it was
the Red Queen.
"She's grown a good deal!"
was her first remark.
She had indeed: when Alice
first found her in the ashes,
she had been
only three inches high—
and here she was,
half a head taller
than Alice herself!

"It's the fresh air that does it,"
said the Rose:
"wonderfully fine air it is,
out here."

"I think I'll go and meet her,"
said Alice, for,
though the flowers
were interesting enough,
she felt that it would be
far grander to have a talk
with a real Queen.

"You can't possibly do that,"
said the Rose:
"I should advise you
to walk the other way."

This sounded nonsense to Alice,
so she said nothing,
but set off at once
towards the Red Queen.
To her surprise,
she lost sight of her in a moment,
and found herself walking
in at the front-door again.

A little provoked, she drew back,
and after looking everywhere
for the queen
(whom she spied out at last,
a long way off), she thought
she would try the plan, this time,
of walking
in the opposite direction.

It succeeded beautifully.
She had not been walking
a minute before she found herself
face to face with the Red Queen,
and full in sight of the hill
she had been so long aiming at.

"Where do you come from?"
said the Red Queen.
"And where are you going?
Look up, speak nicely,
and don't twiddle your fingers
all the time."

Alice attended to all
these directions, and explained,
as well as she could,
that she had lost her way.

"I don't know what you mean
by your way," said the Queen:
"all the ways about here
belong to me — but why did you
come out here at all?"
she added in a kinder tone.
"Curtsey while you're thinking
what to say, it saves time."

Alice wondered a little at this,
but she was too much in awe
of the Queen to disbelieve it.
"I'll try it when I go home,"
she thought to herself,
"the next time
I'm a little late for dinner."

"It's time for you
to answer now," the Queen said,
looking at her watch:
"open your mouth a little wider
when you speak,
and always say 'your Majesty.' "

"I only wanted to see
what the garden was like,
your Majesty —"

"That's right," said the Queen,
patting her on the head,
which Alice didn't like at all,
"though, when you say 'garden,'
— I've seen gardens,
compared with which
this would be a wilderness."

Alice didn't dare
to argue the point, but went on:
"—and I thought I'd try

and find my way
to the top of that hill —"

"When you say 'hill,' "
the Queen interrupted,
"I could show you hills,
in comparison with which
you'd call that a valley."

"No, I shouldn't," said Alice,
surprised into
contradicting her at last:
"a hill can't be a valley,
you know.
That would be nonsense —"

The Red Queen shook her head,
"You may call it 'nonsense'
if you like," she said,
"but I've heard nonsense,
compared with which
that would be
as sensible as a dictionary!"

Alice curtseyed again,
as she was afraid
from the Queen's tone
that she was a little offended:
and they walked on in silence till
they got to the top of the little hill.

For some minutes Alice
stood without speaking,
looking out in all directions
over the country — and
a most curious country it was.
There were a number
of tiny little brooks
running straight across it
from side to side,
and the ground between
was divided up into squares
by a number
of little green hedges,

that reached from brook to brook.

"I declare it's marked out
just like a large chessboard!"
Alice said at last.
"There ought to be some men
moving about somewhere—
and so there are!"
She added in a tone of delight,
and her heart began to beat quick
with excitement as she went on.
"It's a great huge game of chess
that's being played—
all over the world—
if this is the world at all,
you know. Oh, what fun it is!
How I wish I was one of them!
I wouldn't mind being a Pawn,
if only I might join—
though of course
I should like to be a Queen, best."

She glanced rather shyly
at the real Queen as she said this,
but her companion
only smiled pleasantly, and said,
"That's easily managed.
You can be
the White Queen's Pawn,
if you like,
as Lily's too young to play;
and you're in the Second Square
to begin with: when you get
to the Eighth Square
you'll be a Queen—"
Just at this moment,
somehow or other,
they began to run.

Alice never could quite make out,
in thinking it over afterwards,
how it was that they began:
all she remembers is, that they
were running hand in hand,

and the Queen went so fast
that it was all she could do
to keep up with her:
and still the Queen kept crying
"Faster! Faster!" but Alice felt
she could not go faster,
though she had not
breath left to say so.

The most curious part
of the thing was,
that the trees and the other things
round them never changed
their places at all:
however fast they went,
they never seemed
to pass anything.
"I wonder if all the things
move along with us?"
thought poor puzzled Alice.
And the Queen
seemed to guess her thoughts,
for she cried,
"Faster! Don't try to talk!"

Not that Alice
had any idea of doing that.
She felt as if she would never
be able to talk again,
she was getting
so much out of breath:
and still the Queen
cried "Faster! Faster!"
and dragged her along.
"Are we nearly there?"
Alice managed to pant out at last.

"Nearly there!"
the Queen repeated. "Why,
we passed it ten minutes ago!
Faster!" And they ran on
for a time in silence,
with the wind whistling
in Alice's ears,

and almost blowing her hair off
her head, she fancied.

"Now! Now!" cried the Queen.
"Faster! Faster!"
And they went so fast
that at last they seemed
to skim through the air,
hardly touching the ground
with their feet, till suddenly,
just as Alice was getting
quite exhausted, they stopped,
and she found herself
sitting on the ground,
breathless and giddy.

The Queen
propped her up against a tree,
and said kindly,
"You may rest a little now."

Alice looked round her
in great surprise. "Why,
I do believe we've been under
this tree the whole time!
Everything's just as it was!"

"Of course it is," said the Queen,
"what would you have it?"

"Well, in our country,"
said Alice, still panting a little,
"you'd generally
get to somewhere else— if you
ran very fast for a long time,
as we've been doing."

"A slow sort of country!"
said the Queen.
"Now, here, you see,
it takes all the running
you can do,
to keep in the same place.
If you want

to get somewhere else,
you must run at least
twice as fast as that!"

"I'd rather not try, please!"
said Alice.
"I'm quite content to stay here—
only I am so hot and thirsty!"

"I know what you'd like!"
the Queen said good-naturedly,
taking a little box
out of her pocket.
"Have a biscuit?"

Alice thought it would not
be civil to say "No,"
though it wasn't at all
what she wanted. So she took it,
and ate it as well as she could:
and it was very dry; and
she thought she had never been
so nearly choked in all her life.

"While you're
refreshing yourself,"
said the Queen,
"I'll just take the measurements."
And she took a ribbon
out of her pocket,
marked in inches,
and began measuring the ground,
and sticking little pegs
in here and there.

"At the end of two yards,"
she said, putting in a peg
to mark the distance,
"I shall give you your directions
— have another biscuit?"

"No, thank you," said Alice:
"one's quite enough!"

"Thirst quenched, I hope?"
said the Queen.

Alice did not know what to say
to this, but luckily the Queen
did not wait for an answer,
but went on.
"At the end of three yards
I shall repeat them—
for fear of your forgetting them.
At the end of four,
I shall say good-bye.
And at the end of five, I shall go!"

She had got all the pegs put in
by this time, and Alice looked on
with great interest
as she returned to the tree,
and then began slowly
walking down the row.

At the two-yard peg
she faced round, and said,
"A pawn goes two squares
in its first move, you know.
So you'll go very quickly
through the Third Square—
by railway, I should think—
and you'll find yourself
in the Fourth Square in no time.
Well, that square
belongs to Tweedledum
and Tweedledee—
the Fifth is mostly water—
the Sixth belongs
to Humpty Dumpty—
But you make no remark?"

"I—I didn't know
I had to make one—just then,"
Alice faltered out.

"You should have said,
'It's extremely kind of you

to tell me all this'—however,
we'll suppose it said—
the Seventh Square is all forest—
however, one of the Knights
will show you the way—
and in the Eighth Square
we shall be Queens together,
and it's all feasting and fun!"
Alice got up and curtseyed,
and sat down again.

At the next peg
the Queen turned again,
and this time she said,
"Speak in French
when you can't think
of the English for a thing—
turn out your toes as you walk—
and remember who you are!"
She did not wait for Alice
to curtsey this time,
but walked on
quickly to the next peg,
where she turned for a moment
to say "good-bye,"
and then hurried on to the last.

How it happened,
Alice never knew,
but exactly as she came
to the last peg, she was gone.
Whether she vanished
into the air, or whether
she ran quickly into the wood
("and she can run very fast!"
thought Alice),
there was no way of guessing,
but she was gone,
and Alice began to remember
that she was a Pawn,
and that it would soon be
time for her to move

CHAPTER III.

Looking-Glass Insects

Of course the first thing to do
was to make a grand survey
of the country she was
going to travel through.
"It's something
very like learning geography,"
thought Alice,
as she stood on tiptoe in hopes
of being able to see a little further.
"Principal rivers—there are none.
Principal mountains—
I'm on the only one,
but I don't think
it's got any name.
Principal towns—why,
what are those creatures,
making honey down there?
They can't be bees—
nobody ever saw bees a mile off,
you know—" and for some time
she stood silent,
watching one of them
that was bustling
about among the flowers,
poking its proboscis into them,
"just as if it was a regular bee,"
thought Alice.

However, this was anything
but a regular bee:
in fact it was an elephant—
as Alice soon found out,
though the idea quite took her
breath away at first.
"And what enormous flowers
they must be!" was her next idea.
"Something like cottages
with the roofs taken off,
and stalks put to them—
and what quantities of honey

they must make!
I think I'll go down and—no,
I won't just yet," she went on,
checking herself just as she was
beginning to run down the hill,
and trying to find some excuse
for turning shy so suddenly.
"It'll never do to go down
among them without
a good long branch
to brush them away—
and what fun it'll be
when they ask me
how I like my walk.
I shall say—'Oh,
I like it well enough—' "
(here came the favourite
little toss of the head),
" 'only it was so dusty and hot,
and the elephants did tease so!' "

"I think I'll go down
the other way,"
she said after a pause:
"and perhaps I may visit
the elephants later on. Besides,
I do so want
to get into the Third Square!"

So with this excuse
she ran down the hill
and jumped over the first
of the six little brooks.

"Tickets, please!" said the Guard,
putting his head
in at the window.
In a moment everybody
was holding out a ticket:
they were about the same size
as the people, and quite seemed
to fill the carriage.

"Now then! Show your ticket,

child!" the Guard went on,
looking angrily at Alice.
And a great many voices
all said together
("like the chorus of a song,
" thought Alice),
"Don't keep him waiting,
child! Why,
his time is worth
a thousand pounds a minute!"

"I'm afraid I haven't got one,"
Alice said in a frightened tone:
"there wasn't a ticket-office
where I came from."
And again the chorus
of voices went on.
"There wasn't room
for one where she came from.
The land there is worth
a thousand pounds an inch!"

"Don't make excuses,"
said the Guard:
"you should have bought one
from the engine-driver."
And once more the chorus
of voices went on
with "The man that drives
the engine. Why,
the smoke alone is worth
a thousand pounds a puff!"

Alice thought to herself,
"Then there's no use
in speaking."
The voices didn't join in this time,
as she hadn't spoken,
but to her great surprise,
they all thought in chorus
(I hope you understand
what thinking in chorus means—
for I must confess that I don't),
"Better say nothing at all.

Language is worth
a thousand pounds a word!"

"I shall dream
about a thousand pounds tonight,
I know I shall!" thought Alice.

All this time
the Guard was looking at her,
first through a telescope,
then through a microscope,
and then through an opera-glass.
At last he said,
"You're travelling
the wrong way,"
and shut up the window
and went away.

"So young a child,"
said the gentleman
sitting opposite to her
(he was dressed in white paper),
"ought to know
which way she's going,
even if she doesn't know
her own name!"

A Goat,
that was sitting next
to the gentleman in white,
shut his eyes and said
in a loud voice,
"She ought to know her way
to the ticket-office,
even if she doesn't know
her alphabet!"

There was a Beetle
sitting next to the Goat
(it was a very queer carriage-full
of passengers altogether), and,
as the rule seemed to be
that they should all speak in turn,
he went on with

"She'll have to go back
from here as luggage!"

Alice couldn't see
who was sitting
beyond the Beetle,
but a hoarse voice spoke next.
"Change engines—" it said,
and was obliged to leave off.

"It sounds like a horse,"
Alice thought to herself.
And an extremely small voice,
close to her ear, said,
"You might make a joke
on that—
something about 'horse'
and 'hoarse,' you know."

Then a very gentle voice
in the distance said,
"She must be labelled 'Lass,
with care,' you know—"

And after that other voices
went on
("What a number of people
there are in the carriage!"
thought Alice), saying,
"She must go by post,
as she's got a head on her—"
"She must be sent as a message
by the telegraph—"
"She must draw the train herself
the rest of the way—" and so on.

But the gentleman
dressed in white paper
leaned forwards
and whispered in her ear,
"Never mind what they all say,
my dear,
but take a return-ticket
every time the train stops."

"Indeed I shan't!"
Alice said rather impatiently.
"I don't belong
to this railway journey at all—
I was in a wood just now—
and I wish
I could get back there."

"You might make a joke on that,"
said the little voice
close to her ear:
"something about
'you would if you could,'
you know."

"Don't tease so," said Alice,
looking about in vain to see
where the voice came from;
"if you're so anxious
to have a joke made,
why don't you
make one yourself?"

The little voice sighed deeply:
it was very unhappy, evidently,
and Alice would have said
something pitying to comfort it,
"If it would only sigh
like other people!" she thought.
But this was such
a wonderfully small sigh,
that she wouldn't
have heard it at all, if it hadn't
come quite close to her ear.
The consequence of this
was that it tickled her ear
very much,
and quite took off her thoughts
from the unhappiness
of the poor little creature.

"I know you are a friend,"
the little voice went on;

"a dear friend, and an old friend.
And you won't hurt me,
though I am an insect."

"What kind of insect?"
Alice inquired a little anxiously.
What she really
wanted to know was,
whether it could sting or not,
but she thought this wouldn't be
quite a civil question to ask.

"What, then you don't—"
the little voice began,
when it was drowned
by a shrill scream
from the engine,
and everybody jumped up
in alarm, Alice among the rest.

The Horse,
who had put his head out
of the window,
quietly drew it in and said,
"It's only a brook
we have to jump over."
Everybody seemed satisfied
with this,
though Alice felt a little nervous
at the idea
of trains jumping at all.
"However, it'll take us
into the Fourth Square,
that's some comfort!"
she said to herself.
In another moment
she felt the carriage
rise straight up into the air,
and in her fright she caught
at the thing nearest to her hand,
which happened to be
the Goat's beard.

But the beard

seemed to melt away
as she touched it,
and she found herself
sitting quietly under a tree—
while the Gnat
(for that was the insect
she had been talking to)
was balancing itself on a twig
just over her head,
and fanning her with its wings.

It certainly was a very large Gnat:
"about the size of a chicken,"
Alice thought. Still,
she couldn't feel nervous with it,
after they had been
talking together so long.

"—then you
don't like all insects?"
the Gnat went on, as quietly
as if nothing had happened.

"I like them when they can talk,"
Alice said.
"None of them ever talk,
where I come from."

"What sort of insects
do you rejoice in,
where you come from?"
the Gnat inquired.

"I don't rejoice in insects at all,"
Alice explained,
"because I'm rather afraid
of them—at least the large kinds.
But I can tell you
the names of some of them."

"Of course they answer
to their names?"
the Gnat remarked carelessly.

"I never knew them to do it."

"What's the use
of their having names,"
the Gnat said,
"if they won't answer to them?"

"No use to them," said Alice;
"but it's useful
to the people who name them,
I suppose. If not,
why do things
have names at all?"

"I can't say," the Gnat replied.
"Further on,
in the wood down there,
they've got no names—however,
go on with your list of insects:
you're wasting time.
"

"Well, there's the Horse-fly,"
Alice began,
counting off the names
on her fingers.

"All right," said the Gnat:
"half way up that bush,
you'll see a Rocking-horse-fly,
if you look.
It's made entirely of wood,
and gets about by swinging itself
from branch to branch."

"What does it live on?"
Alice asked, with great curiosity.

"Sap and sawdust,"
said the Gnat.
"Go on with the list."

Alice looked up at
the Rocking-horse-fly
with great interest,
and made up her mind
that it must have been
just repainted,
it looked so bright and sticky;
and then she went on.

"And there's the Dragon-fly."

"Look on the branch
above your head," said the Gnat,
"and there you'll find
a snap-dragon-fly. Its body
is made of plum-pudding,
its wings of holly-leaves,
and its head is a raisin
burning in brandy."

"And what does it live on?"

"Frumenty and mince pie,"
the Gnat replied;
"and it makes its nest
in a Christmas box."

"And then there's the Butterfly,"
Alice went on,
after she had taken a good look
at the insect with its head on fire,
and had thought to herself,
"I wonder if that's the reason
insects are so fond of flying
into candles—because they want
to turn into Snap-dragon-flies!"

"Crawling at your feet,"
said the Gnat
(Alice drew her feet back
in some alarm),
"you may observe
a Bread-and-Butterfly.
Its wings are thin slices
of Bread-and-butter,
its body is a crust,

and its head is a lump of sugar."

"And what does it live on?"

"Weak tea with cream in it."

A new difficulty
came into Alice's head.
"Supposing it couldn't find any?"
she suggested.

"Then it would die, of course."

"But that must happen
very often,"
Alice remarked thoughtfully.

"It always happens,"
said the Gnat.

After this, Alice was silent
for a minute or two, pondering.
The Gnat amused itself
meanwhile by humming round
and round her head:
at last it settled
again and remarked,
"I suppose you don't want
to lose your name?"

"No, indeed," Alice said,
a little anxiously.

"And yet I don't know,"
the Gnat went on
in a careless tone:
"only think how convenient
it would be if you could manage
to go home without it!
For instance, if the governess
wanted to call you
to your lessons,
she would call out 'come here—,'
and there she

would have to leave off,
because there wouldn't
be any name for her to call,
and of course you
wouldn't have to go, you know."

"That would never do, I'm sure,"
said Alice:
"the governess would never think
of excusing me lessons for that.
If she couldn't
remember my name,
she'd call me 'Miss!'
as the servants do."

"Well, if she said 'Miss,'
and didn't say anything more,"
the Gnat remarked,
"of course you'd miss
your lessons. That's a joke.
I wish you had made it."

"Why do you wish
I had made it?" Alice asked.
"It's a very bad one."

But the Gnat only sighed deeply,
while two large tears
came rolling down its cheeks.

"You shouldn't make jokes,"
Alice said,
"if it makes you so unhappy."

Then came another
of those melancholy little sighs,
and this time the poor Gnat
really seemed to have
sighed itself away, for,
when Alice looked up,
there was nothing whatever
to be seen on the twig, and,
as she was getting quite chilly
with sitting still so long,

she got up and walked on.

She very soon came
to an open field, with a wood
on the other side of it:
it looked much darker
than the last wood,
and Alice felt a little timid
about going into it. However,
on second thoughts,
she made up her mind to go on:
"for I certainly won't go back,"
she thought to herself,
and this was the only way
to the Eighth Square.

"This must be the wood,"
she said thoughtfully to herself,
"where things have no names.
I wonder what'll become
of my name when I go in?
I shouldn't like to lose it at all—
because they'd have to
give me another,
and it would be
almost certain to be an ugly one.
But then the fun would be trying
to find the creature
that had got my old name!
That's just like
the advertisements, you know,
when people lose dogs—'
answers to the name of "Dash:"
had on a brass collar '—
just fancy calling everything
you met 'Alice,'
till one of them answered!
Only they wouldn't answer at all,
if they were wise."

She was rambling on in this way
when she reached the wood:
it looked very cool and shady.
"Well,

at any rate it's a great comfort,"
she said as she stepped
under the trees,
"after being so hot,
to get into the—into what?"
she went on,
rather surprised at not being able
to think of the word.
"I mean to get under the—
under the—under this,
you know!" putting her hand
on the trunk of the tree.
"What does it call itself,
I wonder?
I do believe it's got no name—
why, to be sure it hasn't!"

She stood silent for a minute,
thinking:
then she suddenly began again.
"Then it really has happened,
after all! And now, who am I?
I will remember, if I can!
I'm determined to do it!"
But being determined
didn't help much,
and all she could say,
after a great deal
of puzzling, was, "L,
I know it begins with L!"

Just then a Fawn
came wandering by:
it looked at Alice
with its large gentle eyes,
but didn't seem at all frightened.
"Here then! Here then!"
Alice said,
as she held out her hand
and tried to stroke it;
but it only started back a little,
and then stood
looking at her again.

"What do you call yourself?"
the Fawn said at last.
Such a soft sweet voice it had!

"I wish I knew!"
thought poor Alice.
She answered, rather sadly,
"Nothing, just now."

"Think again," it said:
"that won't do."

Alice thought,
but nothing came of it. "Please,
would you tell me
what you call yourself?"
she said timidly.
"I think that might help a little."

"I'll tell you,
if you'll move a little further on,"
the Fawn said.
"I can't remember here."

So they walked on together
though the wood,
Alice with her arms
clasped lovingly
round the soft neck of the Fawn,
till they came out
into another open field,
and here the Fawn
gave a sudden bound into the air,
and shook itself free
from Alice's arms. "I'm a Fawn!"
it cried out in a voice of delight,
"and, dear me!
you're a human child!"
A sudden look of alarm came into
its beautiful brown eyes,
and in another moment
it had darted away at full speed.

Alice stood looking after it,

almost ready to cry with vexation
at having lost
her dear little fellow-traveller
so suddenly. "However,
I know my name now." she said,
"that's some comfort. Alice—
Alice—I won't forget it again.
And now,
which of these finger-posts
ought I to follow, I wonder?"

It was not a very difficult
question to answer,
as there was only one road
through the wood,
and the two finger-posts
both pointed along it.
"I'll settle it," Alice said to herself,
"when the road divides
and they point different ways."

But this did not seem
likely to happen.
She went on and on, a long way,
but wherever the road divided
there were sure to be
two finger-posts
pointing the same way,
one marked
"TO TWEEDLEDUM'S HOUSE"
and the other
"TO THE HOUSE
OF TWEEDLEDEE."

"I do believe," said Alice at last,
"that they live in the same house!
I wonder I never thought
of that before—
But I can't stay there long.
I'll just call and say
'how d'you do?' and ask them
the way out of the wood.
If I could only get to
the Eighth Square

before it gets dark!"
So she wandered on,
talking to herself as she went,
till, on turning a sharp corner,
she came upon two fat little men,
so suddenly that she
could not help starting back,
but in another moment
she recovered herself,
feeling sure that they must be.

CHAPTER IV.

Tweedledum
And Tweedledee

They were standing under a tree,
each with an arm
round the other's neck,
and Alice knew
which was which in a moment,
because one of them had "DUM"
embroidered on his collar,
and the other "DEE."
"I suppose they've each got
'TWEEDLE' round
at the back of the collar,"
she said to herself.

They stood so still that she
quite forgot they were alive,
and she was just looking round
to see if the word
'TWEEDLE' was written
at the back of each collar,
when she was startled by a voice
coming from the one
marked "DUM."

"If you think we're wax-works,"
he said, "you ought to pay,
you know.
Wax-works weren't made to be
looked at for nothing, nohow!"

"Contrariwise,"
added the one marked "DEE,"
"if you think we're alive,
you ought to speak."

"I'm sure I'm very sorry,"
was all Alice could say;
for the words of the old song
kept ringing through her head
like the ticking of a clock,

and she could hardly help
saying them out loud:—

"Tweedledum and Tweedledee
  Agreed to have a battle;

For Tweedledum
said Tweedledee
  Had spoiled his nice new rattle.

Just then flew down
a monstrous crow,

  As black as a tar-barrel;

Which frightened
both the heroes so,

  They quite forgot their quarrel."

"I know what
you're thinking about,"
said Tweedledum:
"but it isn't so, nohow."

"Contrariwise,"
continued Tweedledee,
"if it was so, it might be;
and if it were so, it would be;
but as it isn't, it ain't.
That's logic."

"I was thinking,"
Alice said very politely,
"which is the best way out
of this wood: it's getting so dark.
Would you tell me, please?"

But the little men only looked
at each other and grinned.

They looked so exactly
like a couple of great schoolboys,
that Alice couldn't help pointing

her finger at Tweedledum,
and saying "First Boy!"

"Nohow!"
Tweedledum cried out briskly,
and shut his mouth up again
with a snap.

"Next Boy!" said Alice,
passing on to Tweedledee,
though she felt quite certain
he would only shout out
"Contrariwise!" and so he did.

"You've been wrong!"
cried Tweedledum.
"The first thing in a visit
is to say 'How d'ye do?'
and shake hands!"
And here the two brothers
gave each other a hug,
and then they held out
the two hands that were free,
to shake hands with her.

Alice did not like shaking hands
with either of them first,
for fear of hurting
the other one's feelings; so,
as the best way
out of the difficulty,
she took hold
of both hands at once:
the next moment they were
dancing round in a ring.
This seemed quite natural
(she remembered afterwards),
and she was not even surprised
to hear music playing:
it seemed to come from the tree
under which they were dancing,
and it was done
(as well as she could make it out)
by the branches

rubbing one across the other,
like fiddles and fiddle-sticks.

"But it certainly was funny,"
(Alice said afterwards,
when she was telling her sister
the history of all this,)
"to find myself singing
' Here we go round
the mulberry bush.'
I don't know when I began it,
but somehow I felt
as if I'd been singing it
a long long time!"

The other two dancers were fat,
and very soon out of breath.
"Four times round
is enough for one dance,
" Tweedledum panted out,
and they left off dancing
as suddenly as they had begun:
the music stopped
at the same moment.

Then they let go of Alice's hands,
and stood looking at her
for a minute: there was
a rather awkward pause,
as Alice didn't know how to
begin a conversation with people
she had just been dancing with.
"It would never do to say
'How d'ye do?' now,"
she said to herself:
"we seem to have
got beyond that, somehow!"

"I hope you're not much tired?"
she said at last.

"Nohow.
And thank you very much
for asking," said Tweedledum.

"So much obliged!"
added Tweedledee.
"You like poetry?"

"Ye-es,
pretty well— some poetry,"
Alice said doubtfully.
"Would you tell me which road
leads out of the wood?"

"What shall I repeat to her?"
said Tweedledee,
looking round at Tweedledum
with great solemn eyes,
and not noticing Alice's question.

" 'The Walrus and the Carpenter'
is the longest,"
Tweedledum replied,
giving his brother
an affectionate hug.

Tweedledee began instantly:

"The sun was shining—"

Here Alice ventured
to interrupt him.
"If it's very long," she said,
as politely as she could,
"would you please tell me
first which road—"

Tweedledee smiled gently,
and began again:

"The sun was shining on the sea,

 Shining with all his might:

He did his very best to make
 The billows smooth and bright—
And this was odd,

because it was
 The middle of the night.

The moon was shining sulkily,

 Because she thought the sun
Had got no business to be there
 After the day was done—
'It's very rude of him,' she said,

 'To come and spoil the fun!'

The sea was wet as wet could be,

 The sands were dry as dry.

You could not see a cloud,
because
 No cloud was in the sky:

No birds were flying over head—
 There were no birds to fly.

The Walrus and the Carpenter
 Were walking close at hand;

They wept like anything to see
 Such quantities of sand:

'If this were only cleared away,'
They said,'it would be grand!'

'If seven maids with seven mops
 Swept it for half a year,

Do you suppose,'
the Walrus said,

 'That they could get it clear?'
'I doubt it,' said the Carpenter,

 And shed a bitter tear.

'O Oysters,

come and walk with us!'
The Walrus did beseech.

'A pleasant walk,
a pleasant talk,

Along the briny beach:

We cannot do with more than
four,

To give a hand to each.'

The eldest Oyster looked at him.

But never a word he said:

The eldest Oyster winked his eye,

And shook his heavy head—
Meaning to say he did not choose
To leave the oyster-bed.

But four young oysters hurried
up,

All eager for the treat:

Their coats were brushed,
their faces washed,

Their shoes were clean
                and neat—
And this was odd,
because, you know,

They hadn't any feet.

Four other Oysters
followed them,

And yet another four;

And thick and fast

they came at last,

 And more,
and more,
and more—
All hopping
through the frothy waves,

 And scrambling to the shore.

The Walrus and the Carpenter
 Walked on a mile or so,

And then they rested on a rock
 Conveniently low:

And all the little Oysters stood
 And waited in a row.

'The time has come,
' the Walrus said,

'To talk of many things:

Of shoes—and ships—
and sealing-wax—
 Of cabbages—and kings—
And why the sea is boiling hot—
 And whether pigs have wings.
'

'But wait a bit,' the Oysters cried,

'Before we have our chat;

For some of us are out of breath,

 And all of us are fat!'
'No hurry!' said the Carpenter.

 They thanked him much for that.

'A loaf of bread,' the Walrus said,

'Is what we chiefly need:

Pepper and vinegar besides
 Are very good indeed—
Now if you're ready Oysters dear,

 We can begin to feed.'

'But not on us!' the Oysters cried,

 Turning a little blue,

'After such kindness,
that would be
 A dismal thing to do!'
'The night is fine,' the Walrus said
 'Do you admire the view?

'It was so kind of you to come!

 And you are very nice!'
The Carpenter said nothing but
 'Cut us another slice:

I wish you were not
quite so deaf—
 I've had to ask you twice!'

'It seems a shame,'
the Walrus said,

 'To play them such a trick,

After we've
brought them out so far,

 And made them trot so quick!
'
The Carpenter said nothing but
 'The butter's spread too thick!'

'I weep for you,' the Walrus said.

'I deeply sympathize.'

With sobs and tears he sorted out
 Those of the largest size.

Holding his pocket handkerchief
 Before his streaming eyes.

'O Oysters,' said the Carpenter.

 'You've had a pleasant run!

Shall we be trotting home again?'
 But answer came there none—
And that was scarcely odd,
because
 They'd eaten every one."

"I like the Walrus best,"
said Alice:
"because you see he was
a little sorry for the poor oysters."

"He ate more than the Carpenter,
though," said Tweedledee.
"You see he held
his handkerchief in front,
so that the Carpenter
couldn't count how many
he took: contrariwise."

"That was mean!"
Alice said indignantly.
"Then I like the Carpenter best—
if he didn't eat
so many as the Walrus."

"But he ate as many
as he could get,"
said Tweedledum.

This was a puzzler.
After a pause, Alice began,
"Well! They were both
very unpleasant characters—"
Here she checked herself

in some alarm,
at hearing something
that sounded to her like
the puffing of a large
steam-engine
in the wood near them,
though she feared
it was more likely
to be a wild beast.
"Are there any lions
or tigers about here?"
she asked timidly.

"It's only the Red King snoring,"
said Tweedledee.

"Come and look at him!"
the brothers cried,
and they each took one
of Alice's hands,
and led her up to where
the King was sleeping.

"Isn't he a lovely sight?"
said Tweedledum.

Alice couldn't say honestly
that he was.
He had a tall red night-cap on,
with a tassel,
and he was lying crumpled up
into a sort of untidy heap,
and snoring loud—
"fit to snore his head off!"
as Tweedledum remarked.

"I'm afraid he'll catch cold
with lying on the damp grass,"
said Alice,
who was a very thoughtful
little girl.

"He's dreaming now,"
said Tweedledee:

"and what do you think
he's dreaming about?"

Alice said
"Nobody can guess that."

"Why, about you !"
Tweedledee exclaimed,
clapping his hands triumphantly.
"And if he left off
dreaming about you,
where do you suppose you'd be?"

"Where I am now, of course,"
said Alice.

"Not you!" Tweedledee
retorted contemptuously.
"You'd be nowhere. Why,
you're only a sort of thing
in his dream!"

"If that there King was to wake,"
added Tweedledum,
"you'd go out—bang!
—just like a candle!"

"I shouldn't!"
Alice exclaimed indignantly.
"Besides, if I'm only
a sort of thing in his dream,
what are you,
I should like to know?"

"Ditto" said Tweedledum.

"Ditto, ditto" cried Tweedledee.

He shouted this so loud
that Alice couldn't help saying,
"Hush! You'll be waking him,
I'm afraid,
if you make so much noise."

"Well,
it no use your talking about
waking him," said Tweedledum,
"when you're only one
of the things in his dream.
You know very well
you're not real."

"I am real!"
said Alice and began to cry.

"You won't make yourself
a bit realler by crying,"
Tweedledee remarked:
"there's nothing to cry about."

"If I wasn't real," Alice said—
half-laughing through her tears,
it all seemed so ridiculous—
"I shouldn't be able to cry."

"I hope you don't suppose
those are real tears?"
Tweedledum interrupted
in a tone of great contempt.

"I know
they're talking nonsense,"
Alice thought to herself:
"and it's foolish to cry about it."
So she brushed away her tears,
and went on as cheerfully
as she could.
"At any rate I'd better
be getting out of the wood,
for really it's coming on
very dark.
Do you think it's going to rain?"

Tweedledum spread
a large umbrella over himself
and his brother,
and looked up into it.
"No, I don't think it is," he said:

"at least—not under here .
Nohow."

"But it may rain outside?"

"It may—if it chooses,"
said Tweedledee:
"we've no objection.
Contrariwise."

"Selfish things!" thought Alice,
and she was just going to say
"Good-night" and leave them,
when Tweedledum sprang out
from under the umbrella
and seized her by the wrist.

"Do you see that?" he said,
in a voice choking with passion,
and his eyes grew large
and yellow all in a moment,
as he pointed
with a trembling finger
at a small white thing
lying under the tree.

"It's only a rattle," Alice said,
after a careful examination
of the little white thing.
"Not a rattle- snake, you know,"
she added hastily,
thinking that he was frightened:
"only an old rattle—
quite old and broken."

"I knew it was!"
cried Tweedledum,
beginning to stamp about wildly
and tear his hair.
"It's spoilt, of course!"
Here he looked at Tweedledee,
who immediately sat down
on the ground,
and tried to hide himself

under the umbrella.

Alice laid her hand upon his arm,
and said in a soothing tone,
"You needn't be so angry
about an old rattle."

"But it isn't old!"
Tweedledum cried,
in a greater fury than ever.
"It's new, I tell you—
I bought it yesterday—
my nice new RATTLE!"
and his voice rose
to a perfect scream.

All this time Tweedledee
was trying his best
to fold up the umbrella,
with himself in it:
which was such
an extraordinary thing to do,
that it quite took off
Alice's attention
from the angry brother.
But he couldn't quite succeed,
and it ended in his rolling over,
bundled up in the umbrella,
with only his head out:
and there he lay,
opening and shutting his mouth
and his large eyes—
"looking more like a fish
than anything else,"
Alice thought.

"Of course you agree
to have a battle?"
Tweedledum said
in a calmer tone.

"I suppose so,"
the other sulkily replied,
as he crawled out of the umbrella:

"only she must help us
to dress up, you know."

So the two brothers went off
hand-in-hand into the wood,
and returned in a minute
with their arms full of things—
such as bolsters, blankets,
hearth-rugs, table-cloths,
dish-covers and coal-scuttles.
"I hope you're a good hand
at pinning and tying strings?"
Tweedledum remarked.
"Every one of these things
has got to go on,
somehow or other."

Alice said afterwards
she had never seen
such a fuss made about anything
in all her life—
the way those two
bustled about—
and the quantity of things
they put on—
and the trouble they gave her
in tying strings
and fastening buttons—
"Really they'll be more like
bundles of old clothes
than anything else,
by the time they're ready!"
she said to herself,
as she arranged a bolster
round the neck of Tweedledee,
"to keep his head
from being cut off," as he said.

"You know,"
he added very gravely,
"it's one of the most
serious things
that can possibly happen
to one in a battle—

to get one's head cut off."

Alice laughed aloud:
but she managed
to turn it into a cough,
for fear of hurting his feelings.

"Do I look very pale?"
said Tweedledum, coming up
to have his helmet tied on.

(He called it a helmet,
though it certainly
looked much more
like a saucepan.)

"Well—yes—a little,"
Alice replied gently.

"I'm very brave generally,"
he went on in a low voice:
"only to-day I happen
to have a headache."

"And I've got a toothache!"
said Tweedledee,
who had overheard the remark.
"I'm far worse off than you!"

"Then you'd better not fight
to-day," said Alice,
thinking it a good opportunity
to make peace.

"We must have a bit of a fight,
but I don't care
about going on long,"
said Tweedledum.
"What's the time now?"

Tweedledee looked at his watch,
and said "Half-past four."

"Let's fight till six,

and then have dinner,"
said Tweedledum.

"Very well," the other said,
rather sadly:
"and she can watch us—only
you'd better not come very close,"
he added: "I generally hit
everything I can see—
when I get really excited."

"And I hit everything
within reach," cried Tweedledum,
"whether I can see it or not!"

Alice laughed.
"You must hit the trees
pretty often, I should think,"
she said.

Tweedledum looked round him
with a satisfied smile.
"I don't suppose," he said,
"there'll be a tree left standing,
for ever so far round,
by the time we've finished!"

"And all about a rattle!"
said Alice, still hoping
to make them a little ashamed
of fighting for such a trifle.

"I shouldn't have
minded it so much,"
said Tweedledum,
"if it hadn't been a new one."

"I wish the monstrous crow
would come!" thought Alice.

"There's only one sword,
you know,"
Tweedledum said to his brother:
"but you can have the umbrella—

it's quite as sharp.
Only we must begin quick.
It's getting as dark as it can."

"And darker," said Tweedledee.

It was getting dark so suddenly
that Alice thought there must be
a thunderstorm coming on.
"What a thick black cloud
that is!" she said.
"And how fast it comes! Why,
I do believe it's got wings!"

"It's the crow!"
Tweedledum cried out
in a shrill voice of alarm:
and the two brothers
took to their heels
and were out of sight
in a moment.

Alice ran a little way
into the wood,
and stopped under a large tree.
"It can never get at me here,"
she thought: "it's far too large
to squeeze itself
in among the trees.
But I wish it wouldn't
flap its wings so—
it makes quite a hurricane
in the wood—
here's somebody's shawl
being blown away!"

CHAPTER V.

Wool and Water

She caught the shawl
as she spoke,
and looked about for the owner:
in another moment
the White Queen
came running wildly
through the wood,
with both arms
stretched out wide,
as if she were flying,
and Alice very civilly
went to meet her with the shawl.

"I'm very glad I happened
to be in the way," Alice said,
as she helped her
to put on her shawl again.

The White Queen only looked
at her in a helpless frightened
sort of way,
and kept repeating something
in a whisper to herself
that sounded like
"bread-and-butter,
bread-and-butter,"
and Alice felt that if there was
to be any conversation at all,
she must manage it herself.
So she began rather timidly:
"Am I addressing
the White Queen?"

"Well, yes,
if you call that a-dressing,"
The Queen said.
"It isn't my notion of the thing,
at all."

Alice thought it would never do

to have an argument
at the very beginning
of their conversation,
so she smiled and said,
"If your Majesty will only tell me
the right way to begin,
I'll do it as well as I can."

"But I don't want it done at all!"
groaned the poor Queen.
"I've been a-dressing myself
for the last two hours."

It would have been all the better,
as it seemed to Alice,
if she had got some one else
to dress her,
she was so dreadfully untidy.
"Every single thing's crooked,"
Alice thought to herself,
"and she's all over pins! —
may I put your shawl straight
for you?" she added aloud.

"I don't know
what's the matter with it!"
the Queen said,
in a melancholy voice.
"It's out of temper,
I think. I've pinned it here,
and I've pinned it there,
but there's no pleasing it!"

"It can't go straight, you know,
if you pin it all on one side,"
Alice said,
as she gently put it right for her;
"and, dear me,
what a state your hair is in!"

"The brush
has got entangled in it!"
the Queen said with a sigh.
"And I lost the comb yesterday."

Alice carefully released the brush,
and did her best
to get the hair into order.
"Come,
you look rather better now!"
she said,
after altering most of the pins.
"But really you should have
a lady's maid!"

"I'm sure I'll take you with
pleasure!" the Queen said.
"Twopence a week,
and jam every other day."

Alice couldn't help laughing,
as she said,
"I don't want you to hire me —
and I don't care for jam."

"It's very good jam,"
said the Queen.

"Well, I don't want any to-day,
at any rate."

"You couldn't have it
if you did want it,"
the Queen said. "The rule is,
jam to-morrow
and jam yesterday—
but never jam to-day."

"It must come sometimes
to 'jam to-day,' " Alice objected.

"No, it can't," said the Queen.
"It's jam every other day:
to-day isn't any other day,
you know."

"I don't understand you,"
said Alice.

"It's dreadfully confusing!"

"That's the effect
of living backwards,"
the Queen said kindly:
"it always makes one
a little giddy at first—"

"Living backwards!"
Alice repeated
in great astonishment.
"I never heard of such a thing!"

"—but there's
one great advantage in it,
that one's memory works
both ways."

"I'm sure mine only works
one way," Alice remarked.
"I can't remember things
before they happen."

"It's a poor sort of memory
that only works backwards,"
the Queen remarked.

"What sort of things
do you remember best?"
Alice ventured to ask.

"Oh,
things that happened
the week after next,"
the Queen replied
in a careless tone.
"For instance, now," she went on,
sticking a large piece of plaster
on her finger as she spoke,
"there's the King's Messenger.
He's in prison now,
being punished:
and the trial doesn't even begin
till next Wednesday:

and of course
the crime comes last of all."

"Suppose
he never commits the crime?"
said Alice.

"That would be all the better,
wouldn't it?" the Queen said,
as she bound the plaster
round her finger
with a bit of ribbon.

Alice
felt there was no denying that .
"Of course it would be
all the better," she said:
"but it wouldn't be all the better
his being punished."

"You're wrong there,
at any rate," said the Queen:
"were you ever punished?"

"Only for faults," said Alice.

"And you were
all the better for it, I know!"
the Queen said triumphantly.

"Yes,
but then I had done the things
I was punished for," said Alice:
"that makes all the difference."

"But if you hadn't done them,"
the Queen said,
"that would have been better still;
better, and better, and better!"
Her voice went higher
with each "better,"
till it got quite to a squeak at last.

Alice was just beginning to say

"There's a mistake
somewhere—,"
when the Queen
began screaming so loud
that she had to leave
the sentence unfinished.
"Oh, oh, oh!" shouted the Queen,
shaking her hand about
as if she wanted to shake it off.
"My finger's bleeding!
Oh, oh, oh, oh!"

Her screams were so exactly
like the whistle of a steam-engine,
that Alice had to hold
both her hands over her ears.

"What is the matter?" she said,
as soon as there was
a chance of making herself heard.
"Have you pricked your finger?"

"I haven't pricked it yet,"
the Queen said,
"but I soon shall—oh, oh, oh!"

"When do you expect to do it?"
Alice asked,
feeling very much inclined
to laugh.

"When I fasten my shawl again,"
the poor Queen groaned out:
"the brooch
will come undone directly.
Oh, oh!"
As she said the words
the brooch flew open,
and the Queen
clutched wildly at it,
and tried to clasp it again.

"Take care!" cried Alice.
"You're holding it all crooked!"

And she caught at the brooch;
but it was too late:
the pin had slipped,
and the Queen
had pricked her finger.

"That accounts for the bleeding,
you see,"
she said to Alice with a smile.
"Now you understand
the way things happen here."

"But why don't you
scream now?" Alice asked,
holding her hands
ready to put over her ears again.

"Why, I've done
all the screaming already,"
said the Queen.
"What would be the good
of having it all over again?"

By this time it was getting light.
"The crow
must have flown away, I think,"
said Alice: "I'm so glad it's gone.
I thought
it was the night coming on."

"I wish I could manage
to be glad!" the Queen said.
"Only I never can remember
the rule.
You must be very happy,
living in this wood,
and being glad
whenever you like!"

"Only it is so very lonely here!"
Alice said in a melancholy voice;
and at the thought
of her loneliness two large tears
came rolling down her cheeks.

"Oh, don't go on like that!"
cried the poor Queen,
wringing her hands in despair.
"Consider
what a great girl you are.
Consider what a long way
you've come to-day.
Consider what o'clock it is.
Consider anything,
only don't cry!"

Alice
could not help laughing at this,
even in the midst of her tears.
"Can you keep from crying
by considering things?"
she asked.

"That's the way it's done,"
the Queen said
with great decision:
"nobody can do two things
at once, you know.
Let's consider your age
to begin with—how old are you?"

"I'm seven and a half exactly."

"You needn't say 'exactually,' "
the Queen remarked:
"I can believe it without that.
Now I'll give you
something to believe.
I'm just one hundred and one,
five months and a day."

"I can't believe that !" said Alice.

"Can't you?"
the Queen said in a pitying tone.
"Try again: draw a long breath,
and shut your eyes."

Alice laughed.
"There's no use trying," she said:
"one can't believe
impossible things."

"I daresay
you haven't had much practice,"
said the Queen.
"When I was your age,
I always did it
for half-an-hour a day. Why,
sometimes I've believed
as many as six impossible things
before breakfast.
There goes the shawl again!"

The brooch had come undone
as she spoke,
and a sudden gust of wind
blew the Queen's shawl
across a little brook.
The Queen
spread out her arms again,
and went flying after it,
and this time she succeeded
in catching it for herself.
"I've got it!"
she cried in a triumphant tone.
"Now you shall see me
pin it on again, all by myself!"

"Then I hope your finger
is better now?"
Alice said very politely,
as she crossed the little brook
after the Queen.

"Oh, much better!"
cried the Queen,
her voice rising to a squeak
as she went on. "Much be-etter!
Be-etter! Be-e-e-etter! Be-e-ehh!"
The last word ended
in a long bleat,

so like a sheep
that Alice quite started.

She looked at the Queen,
who seemed to have suddenly
wrapped herself up in wool.
Alice rubbed her eyes,
and looked again.
She couldn't make out
what had happened at all.
Was she in a shop?
And was that really—
was it really a sheep
that was sitting
on the other side of the counter?
Rub as she could,
she could make nothing more
of it: she was in a little dark shop,
leaning with her elbows
on the counter,
and opposite to her
was an old Sheep,
sitting in an arm-chair knitting,
and every now and then
leaving off to look at her
through a great pair of spectacles.

"What is it you want to buy?"
the Sheep said at last,
looking up for a moment
from her knitting.

"I don't quite know yet,"
Alice said, very gently.
"I should like
to look all round me first,
if I might."

"You may look in front of you,
and on both sides, if you like,"
said the Sheep:
"but you can't look
all round you—
unless you've got eyes

at the back of your head."

But these, as it happened,
Alice had not got:
so she contented herself
with turning round,
looking at the shelves
as she came to them.

The shop seemed to be full
of all manner of curious things—
but the oddest part of it all was,
that whenever
she looked hard at any shelf,
to make out exactly
what it had on it,
that particular shelf
was always quite empty:
though the others round it
were crowded as full
as they could hold.

"Things flow about so here!"
she said at last in a plaintive tone,
after she had spent a minute or so
in vainly pursuing
a large bright thing,
that looked sometimes like a doll
and sometimes like a work-box,
and was always in the shelf
next above the one
she was looking at.
"And this one
is the most provoking of all—
but I'll tell you what—"
she added,
as a sudden thought struck her,
"I'll follow it up
to the very top shelf of all.
It'll puzzle it
to go through the ceiling,
I expect!"

But even this plan failed:

the "thing"
went through the ceiling
as quietly as possible,
as if it were quite used to it.

"Are you a child or a teetotum?"
the Sheep said,
as she took up
another pair of needles.
"You'll make me giddy soon,
if you go on
turning round like that."
She was now working
with fourteen pairs at once,
and Alice couldn't help
looking at her
in great astonishment.

"How can she knit
with so many?" the puzzled child
thought to herself.
"She gets more and more
like a porcupine every minute!"

"Can you row?" the Sheep asked,
handing her a pair
of knitting-needles as she spoke.

"Yes, a little—but not on land—
and not with needles—"
Alice was beginning to say,
when suddenly the needles
turned into oars in her hands,
and she found
they were in a little boat,
gliding along between banks:
so there was nothing
for it but to do her best.

"Feather!" cried the Sheep,
as she took up
another pair of needles.

This didn't sound like a remark

that needed any answer,
so Alice said nothing,
but pulled away.
There was something very queer
about the water, she thought,
as every now and then
the oars got fast in it,
and would hardly
come out again.

"Feather! Feather!"
the Sheep cried again,
taking more needles.
"You'll be catching
a crab directly."

"A dear little crab!" thought Alice.
"I should like that."

"Didn't you hear me say
'Feather'?"
the Sheep cried angrily,
taking up
quite a bunch of needles.

"Indeed I did," said Alice:
"you've said it very often—
and very loud. Please,
where are the crabs?"

"In the water, of course!"
said the Sheep, sticking some
of the needles into her hair,
as her hands were full.
"Feather, I say!"

"Why do you say 'feather'
so often?" Alice asked at last,
rather vexed. "I'm not a bird!"

"You are," said the Sheep:
"you're a little goose."

This offended Alice a little,

so there was no more
conversation for a minute or two,
while the boat glided gently on,
sometimes among beds of weeds
(which made the oars
stick fast in the water,
worse then ever),
and sometimes under trees,
but always with
the same tall river-banks
frowning over their heads.

"Oh, please!
There are some scented rushes!"
Alice cried
in a sudden transport of delight.
"There really are—
and such beauties!"

"You needn't say 'please'
to me about "em," the Sheep said,
without looking up
from her knitting:
"I didn't put "em there,
and I'm not going
to take "em away."

"No, but I meant—please,
may we wait and pick some?"
Alice pleaded.
"If you don't mind
stopping the boat for a minute."

"How am I to stop it?"
said the Sheep.
"If you leave off rowing,
it'll stop of itself."

So the boat was left
to drift down the stream
as it would,
till it glided gently
in among the waving rushes.
And then the little sleeves

were carefully rolled up,
and the little arms were plunged
in elbow-deep to get the rushes
a good long way down
before breaking them off —
and for a while Alice forgot
all about the Sheep
and the knitting, as she bent over
the side of the boat,
with just the ends
of her tangled hair
dipping into the water —
while with bright eager eyes
she caught at
one bunch after another
of the darling scented rushes.

"I only hope the boat
won't tipple over!"
she said to herself. "Oh,
what a lovely one!
Only I couldn't quite reach it."
"And it certainly did seem
a little provoking
("almost as if it happened
on purpose," she thought) that,
though she managed
to pick plenty of beautiful rushes
as the boat glided by,
there was always
a more lovely one
that she couldn't reach.

"The prettiest
are always further!"
she said at last,
with a sigh at the obstinacy
of the rushes
in growing so far off,
as, with flushed cheeks
and dripping hair and hands,
she scrambled back
into her place,
and began to arrange

her new-found treasures.

What mattered it to her just then
that the rushes had begun to fade,
and to lose all their scent
and beauty,
from the very moment
that she picked them?
Even real scented rushes,
you know,
last only a very little while —
and these, being dream-rushes,
melted away almost like snow,
as they lay in heaps at her feet —
but Alice hardly noticed this,
there were so many
other curious things
to think about.

They hadn't gone much farther
before the blade of one of the oars
got fast in the water
and wouldn't come out again
(so Alice explained it afterwards),
and the consequence
was that the handle of it
caught her under the chin, and,
in spite of a series of little shrieks
of "Oh, oh, oh!" from poor Alice,
it swept her straight off the seat,
and down
among the heap of rushes.

However, she wasn't hurt,
and was soon up again:
the Sheep went on
with her knitting all the while,
just as if nothing had happened.
"That was a nice crab
you caught!" she remarked,
as Alice got back into her place,
very much relieved
to find herself still in the boat.

"Was it? I didn't see it,"
said Alice, peeping cautiously
over the side of the boat
into the dark water.
"I wish it hadn't let go—
I should so like to see a little crab
to take home with me!"
But the Sheep
only laughed scornfully,
and went on with her knitting.

"Are there many crabs here?"
said Alice.

"Crabs, and all sorts of things,"
said the Sheep:
"plenty of choice,
only make up your mind.
Now, what do you want to buy?"

"To buy!" Alice echoed in a tone
that was half astonished
and half frightened—for the oars,
and the boat, and the river,
had vanished all in a moment,
and she was back again
in the little dark shop.

"I should like to buy an egg,
please," she said timidly.
"How do you sell them?"

"Fivepence farthing for one—
Twopence for two,"
the Sheep replied.

"Then two
are cheaper than one?"
Alice said in a surprised tone,
taking out her purse.

"Only you must eat them both,
if you buy two," said the Sheep.

"Then I'll have one, please,"
said Alice, as she put
the money down on the counter.
For she thought to herself,
"They mightn't be at all nice,
you know."

The Sheep took the money,
and put it away in a box:
then she said "I never put things
into people's hands—
that would never do—
you must get it for yourself."
And so saying, she went off
to the other end of the shop,
and set the egg upright on a shelf.

"I wonder why it wouldn't do?"
thought Alice,
as she groped her way
among the tables and chairs,
for the shop was very dark
towards the end.
"The egg seems to get
further away
the more I walk towards it.
Let me see, is this a chair?
Why, it's got branches, I declare!
How very odd
to find trees growing here!
And actually here's a little brook!
Well,
this is the very queerest shop
I ever saw!"

So she went on,
wondering more and more
at every step,
as everything turned into a tree
the moment she came up to it,
and she quite expected
the egg to do the same.

CHAPTER VI.

Humpty Dumpty

However,
the egg only got larger and larger,
and more and more human:
when she had come
within a few yards of it,
she saw that it had eyes
and a nose and mouth;
and when she had
come close to it,
she saw clearly that it was
HUMPTY DUMPTY himself.
"It can't be anybody else!"
she said to herself.
"I'm as certain of it,
as if his name
were written all over his face."

It might have been written
a hundred times, easily,
on that enormous face.
Humpty Dumpty was sitting
with his legs crossed, like a Turk,
on the top of a high wall—
such a narrow one
that Alice quite wondered how
he could keep his balance—and,
as his eyes were steadily fixed
in the opposite direction,
and he didn't take
the least notice of her,
she thought he must
be a stuffed figure after all.

"And how exactly like an egg
he is!" she said aloud,
standing with her hands
ready to catch him,
for she was every moment
expecting him to fall.

"It's very provoking,"
Humpty Dumpty
said after a long silence,
looking away from Alice
as he spoke,
"to be called an egg— Very!"

"I said you looked like an egg,
Sir," Alice gently explained.
"And some eggs are very pretty,
you know" she added,
hoping to turn her remark
into a sort of a compliment.

"Some people,"
said Humpty Dumpty,
looking away from her as usual,
"have no more sense
than a baby!"

Alice didn't know
what to say to this:
it wasn't at all like conversation,
she thought,
as he never said anything to her ;
in fact,
his last remark was evidently
addressed to a tree—
so she stood
and softly repeated to herself:—

"Humpty Dumpty sat on a wall:
Humpty Dumpty had a great fall.
All the King's horses
and all the King's men
Couldn't put Humpty Dumpty
in his place again."

"That last line
is much too long for the poetry,"
she added, almost out loud,
forgetting that Humpty Dumpty
would hear her.

"Don't stand there
chattering to yourself like that,"
Humpty Dumpty said,
looking at her for the first time,
"but tell me your name
and your business."

"My name is Alice, but—"

"It's a stupid enough name!"
Humpty Dumpty
interrupted impatiently.

"What does it mean?"

"Must a name mean something?"
Alice asked doubtfully.

"Of course it must,"
Humpty Dumpty
said with a short laugh:
"my name means
the shape I am—
and a good handsome shape it is,
too. With a name like yours,
you might be any shape, almost."

"Why do you sit out here
all alone?" said Alice,
not wishing
to begin an argument.

"Why,
because there's nobody with me!"
cried Humpty Dumpty.
"Did you think I didn't know the
answer to that? Ask another."

"Don't you think you'd be safer
down on the ground?"
Alice went on,
not with any idea
of making another riddle,
but simply in her

good-natured anxiety
for the queer creature.
"That wall is so very narrow!"

"What tremendously
easy riddles you ask!"
Humpty Dumpty growled out.
"Of course I don't think so!
Why, if ever I did fall off—
which there's no chance of—
but if I did—"
Here he pursed his lips
and looked so solemn and grand
that Alice
could hardly help laughing.
"If I did fall," he went on,
"The King has promised me—
with his very own mouth —
to—to—"

"To send all his horses
and all his men,"
Alice interrupted,
rather unwisely.

"Now I declare that's too bad!"
Humpty Dumpty cried,
breaking into a sudden passion.
"You've been listening at doors—
and behind trees—
and down chimneys—
or you couldn't have known it!"

"I haven't, indeed!"
Alice said very gently.
"It's in a book."

"Ah, well!
They may write
such things in a book,"
Humpty Dumpty
said in a calmer tone.
"That's what you call
a History of England, that is.

Now, take a good look at me!
I'm one that has spoken to a King,
I am: mayhap you'll never see
such another:
and to show you I'm not proud,
you may shake hands with me!"
And he grinned
almost from ear to ear,
as he leant forwards
(and as nearly as possible
fell off the wall in doing so)
and offered Alice his hand.
She watched him
a little anxiously as she took it.
"If he smiled much more,
the ends of his mouth
might meet behind," she thought:
"and then I don't know
what would happen to his head!
I'm afraid it would come off!"

"Yes, all his horses
and all his men,"
Humpty Dumpty went on.
"They'd pick me up again
in a minute, they would!
However, this conversation
is going on a little too fast:
let's go back
to the last remark but one."

"I'm afraid
I can't quite remember it,"
Alice said very politely.

"In that case we start fresh,"
said Humpty Dumpty,
"and it's my turn
to choose a subject—"
("He talks about it
just as if it was a game!"
thought Alice.)
"So here's a question for you.
How old did you say you were?"

Alice made a short calculation,
and said
"Seven years and six months."

"Wrong!" Humpty Dumpty
exclaimed triumphantly.
"You never said a word like it!"

"I though you meant
'How old are you?' "
Alice explained.

"If I'd meant that,
I'd have said it,"
said Humpty Dumpty.

Alice didn't want to begin
another argument,
so she said nothing.

"Seven years and six months!"
Humpty Dumpty
repeated thoughtfully.
"An uncomfortable sort of age.
Now if you'd asked my advice,
I'd have said 'Leave off
at seven'—but it's too late now."

"I never ask advice
about growing,"
Alice said indignantly.

"Too proud?" the other inquired.

Alice felt even more indignant
at this suggestion.
"I mean," she said,
"that one can't help
growing older."

"One can't, perhaps,"
said Humpty Dumpty,
"but two can.

With proper assistance,
you might have left off at seven."

"What a beautiful belt
you've got on!"
Alice suddenly remarked.

(They had had quite enough
of the subject of age,
she thought:
and if they really were
to take turns in choosing subjects,
it was her turn now.) "At least,"
she corrected herself
on second thoughts,
"a beautiful cravat,
I should have said—no, a belt,
I mean—I beg your pardon!"
she added in dismay,
for Humpty Dumpty
looked thoroughly offended,
and she began to wish
she hadn't chosen that subject.
"If I only knew,"
she thought to herself,
"which was neck
and which was waist!"

Evidently Humpty Dumpty
was very angry,
though he said nothing
for a minute or two.
When he did speak again,
it was in a deep growl.

"It is a— most—
provoking —thing,"
he said at last,
"when a person doesn't know
a cravat from a belt!"

"I know it's very ignorant of me,"
Alice said, in so humble a tone
that Humpty Dumpty relented.

"It's a cravat, child,
and a beautiful one, as you say.
It's a present from
the White King and Queen.
There now!"

"Is it really?" said Alice,
quite pleased to find
that she had chosen
a good subject, after all.

"They gave it me,"
Humpty Dumpty
continued thoughtfully,
as he crossed one knee
over the other
and clasped his hands round it,
"they gave it me—
for an un-birthday present."

"I beg your pardon?"
Alice said with a puzzled air.

"I'm not offended,"
said Humpty Dumpty.

"I mean,
what is an un-birthday present?"

"A present given
when it isn't your birthday,
of course."

Alice considered a little.
"I like birthday presents best,"
she said at last.

"You don't know
what you're talking about!"
cried Humpty Dumpty.
"How many days
are there in a year?"

"Three hundred and sixty-five,"
said Alice.

"And how many birthdays
have you?"

"One."

"And if you take one
from three hundred
and sixty-five, what remains?"

"Three hundred
and sixty-four, of course."

Humpty Dumpty
looked doubtful.
"I'd rather see that
done on paper," he said.

Alice couldn't help smiling
as she took out
her memorandum-book,
and worked the sum for him:

365
  1

364

Humpty Dumpty took the book,
and looked at it carefully.
"That seems to be done right—"
he began.

"You're holding it upside down!"
Alice interrupted.

"To be sure I was!"
Humpty Dumpty said gaily,
as she turned it round for him.
"I thought it looked a little queer.
As I was saying,
that seems to be done right—

though I haven't time to look
it over thoroughly just now—
and that shows that there are
three hundred
and sixty-four days
when you might get
un-birthday presents—"

"Certainly," said Alice.

"And only one
for birthday presents,
you know. There's glory for you!"

"I don't know what you mean
by 'glory,' " Alice said.

Humpty Dumpty
smiled contemptuously.
"Of course you don't—
till I tell you.
I meant '
there's a nice knock-down
argument for you!' "

"But 'glory' doesn't mean
'a nice knock-down argument,' "
Alice objected.

"When I use a word,"
Humpty Dumpty
said in rather a scornful tone,
"it means just what I choose it
to mean—neither more nor less."

"The question is," said Alice,
"whether you can make words
mean so many different things."

"The question is,"
said Humpty Dumpty,
"which is to be master—
that's all."

Alice was too much puzzled
to say anything, so after a minute
Humpty Dumpty began again.
"They've a temper,
some of them—particularly verbs,
they're the proudest—adjectives
you can do anything with,
but not verbs—however,
I can manage the whole lot
of them! Impenetrability!
That's what I say!"

"Would you tell me, please,"
said Alice "what that means?"

"Now you talk
like a reasonable child,"
said Humpty Dumpty,
looking very much pleased.
"I meant by 'impenetrability'
that we've had enough
of that subject,
and it would be just as well
if you'd mention
what you mean to do next,
as I suppose you don't mean
to stop here all the rest
of your life."

"That's a great deal
to make one word mean,"
Alice said in a thoughtful tone.

"When I make a word
do a lot of work like that,"
said Humpty Dumpty,
"I always pay it extra."

"Oh!" said Alice.
She was too much puzzled
to make any other remark.

"Ah, you should see
"em come round me

of a Saturday night,"
Humpty Dumpty went on,
wagging his head gravely
from side to side:
"for to get their wages,
you know."

(Alice didn't venture
to ask what he paid them with;
and so you see I can't tell you .)

"You seem very clever
at explaining words,
Sir," said Alice.
"Would you kindly tell me
the meaning of the poem
called 'Jabberwocky'?"

"Let's hear it,"
said Humpty Dumpty.
"I can explain all the poems
that were ever invented—
and a good many that haven't
been invented just yet."

This sounded very hopeful,
so Alice repeated the first verse:

'Twas brillig, and the slithy toves
Did gyre and gimble in the wabe;

All mimsy were the borogoves,

 And the mome raths outgrabe.

"That's enough to begin with,"
Humpty Dumpty interrupted:
"there are plenty
of hard words there.
' Brillig ' means four o'clock
in the afternoon—
the time when
you begin broiling things
for dinner."

"That'll do very well," said Alice:
"and 'slithy'?"

"Well,
' slithy ' means 'lithe and slimy.
' 'Lithe' is the same as 'active.'
You see it's like a portmanteau—
there are two meanings
packed up into one word."

"I see it now,"
Alice remarked thoughtfully:
"and what are ' toves '?"

"Well,' toves '
are something like badgers—
they're something like lizards—
and they're something like
corkscrews."

"They must be
very curious looking creatures."

"They are that,"
said Humpty Dumpty:
"also they make their nests
under sun-dials—
also they live on cheese."

"And what's the ' gyre '
and to ' gimble '?"

"To ' gyre ' is to go round
and round like a gyroscope.
To ' gimble ' is to make holes
like a gimlet."

"And ' the wabe '
is the grass-plot round a sun-dial,
I suppose?" said Alice,
surprised at her own ingenuity.

"Of course it is. It's called ' wabe,'
you know,
because it goes a long way
before it,
and a long way behind it—"

"And a long way beyond it
on each side," Alice added.

"Exactly so. Well, then,
' mimsy ' is 'flimsy
and miserable'
(there's another portmanteau
for you).
And a ' borogove ' is a thin
shabby-looking bird
with its feathers sticking out
all round—
something like a live mop."

"And then ' mome raths '?"
said Alice.
"I'm afraid I'm giving you
a great deal of trouble."

"Well,
a ' rath ' is a sort of green pig:
but ' mome '
I'm not certain about.
I think it's short for
'from home'—
meaning that they'd lost
their way, you know."

"And what does
' outgrabe ' mean?"

"Well, ' outgrabing ' is something
between bellowing and whistling,
with a kind of sneeze
in the middle: however,
you'll hear it done, maybe—
down in the wood yonder—
and when you've once heard it
you'll be quite content.

Who's been repeating
all that hard stuff to you?"

"I read it in a book," said Alice.
"But I had some poetry
repeated to me,
much easier than that,
by—Tweedledee, I think it was."

"As to poetry, you know,"
said Humpty Dumpty,
stretching out
one of his great hands,
"I can repeat poetry
as well as other folk,
if it comes to that—"

"Oh, it needn't come to that!"
Alice hastily said, hoping
to keep him from beginning.

"The piece I'm going to repeat,"
he went on
without noticing her remark,
"was written entirely
for your amusement."

Alice felt that in that case
she really ought to listen to it,
so she sat down, and said
"Thank you" rather sadly.

"In winter,
when the fields are white,
I sing this song for your delight—

only I don't sing it,"
he added, as an explanation.

"I see you don't," said Alice.

"If you can see whether
I'm singing or not,
you've sharper eyes than most."

Humpty Dumpty
remarked severely.
Alice was silent.

"In spring,
when woods are getting green,
I'll try and tell you what I mean."

"Thank you very much,"
said Alice.

"In summer,
when the days are long,

Perhaps you'll understand
 the song:

In autumn,
when the leaves are brown,

Take pen and ink,
and write it down."

"I will,
if I can remember it so long,"
said Alice.

"You needn't go
on making remarks like that,"
Humpty Dumpty said:

"they're not sensible,
and they put me out."

"I sent a message to the fish:

I told them 'This is what I wish.'

The little fishes of the sea,

They sent an answer back to me.

The little fishes' answer
was 'We cannot do it,

Sir, because—'"

"I'm afraid
I don't quite understand,"
said Alice.

"It gets easier further on,"
Humpty Dumpty replied.

"I sent to them again to say
'It will be better to obey.'

The fishes answered with a grin,

'Why, what a temper you are in!'

I told them once,
I told them twice:

They would not listen to advice.

I took a kettle large and new,

Fit for the deed I had to do.

My heart went hop,
my heart went thump;

I filled the kettle at the pump.

Then some one came to me
and said,

'The little fishes are in bed.'

I said to him, I said it plain,

'Then you must
wake them up again.'

I said it very loud and clear;

I went and shouted in his ear."

Humpty Dumpty raised his voice
almost to a scream
as he repeated this verse,
and Alice thought
with a shudder,
"I wouldn't have been
the messenger for anything !"

"But he was very stiff and proud;

He said
'You needn't shout so loud!'

And he was very proud and stiff;

He said 'I'd go and wake them,
if—'

I took a corkscrew from the shelf:

I went to wake them up myself.

And when I found the door
was locked,

I pulled and pushed
and kicked and knocked.

And when I found the door
was shut,

I tried to turn the handle,
but—"

There was a long pause.

"Is that all?" Alice timidly asked.

"That's all,"
said Humpty Dumpty.
"Good-bye."

This was rather sudden,
Alice thought: but,

after such a very strong hint
that she ought to be going,
she felt that it would hardly be
civil to stay. So she got up,
and held out her hand.
"Good-bye, till we meet again!"
she said as cheerfully
as she could.

"I shouldn't know you again
if we did meet,"
Humpty Dumpty replied
in a discontented tone,
giving her one of his fingers
to shake;
"you're so exactly
like other people."

"The face is what one goes by,
generally," Alice remarked
in a thoughtful tone.

"That's just what I complain of,"
said Humpty Dumpty.
"Your face is the same
as everybody has—the two eyes,
so—" (marking their places
in the air with this thumb)
"nose in the middle,
mouth under.
It's always the same.
Now if you had the two eyes
on the same side of the nose,
for instance—
or the mouth at the top—
that would be some help."

"It wouldn't look nice,"
Alice objected.
But Humpty Dumpty
only shut his eyes
and said "Wait till you've tried."

Alice waited a minute

to see if he would speak again,
but as he never opened his eyes
or took any further notice of her,
she said "Good-bye!" once more,
and, getting no answer to this,
she quietly walked away:
but she couldn't help saying
to herself as she went,
"Of all the unsatisfactory—"
(she repeated this aloud,
as it was a great comfort
to have such a long word to say)
"of all the unsatisfactory people
I ever met—"
She never finished the sentence,
for at this moment a heavy crash
shook the forest from end to end.

CHAPTER VII.

The Lion and the Unicorn

The next moment soldiers
came running through the wood,
at first in twos and threes,
then ten or twenty together,
and at last in such crowds
that they seemed
to fill the whole forest.
Alice got behind a tree,
for fear of being run over,
and watched them go by.

She thought that in all her life
she had never seen soldiers
so uncertain on their feet:
they were always tripping over
something or other,
and whenever one went down,
several more
always fell over him,
so that the ground was soon
covered with little heaps of men.

Then came the horses.
Having four feet,
these managed rather better
than the foot-soldiers:
but even they stumbled
now and then; and it seemed
to be a regular rule that,
whenever a horse stumbled
the rider fell off instantly.
The confusion
got worse every moment,
and Alice was very glad
to get out of the wood
into an open place,
where she found the White King
seated on the ground,
busily writing in his
memorandum-book.

"I've sent them all!"
the King cried
in a tone of delight,
on seeing Alice.
"Did you happen to meet
any soldiers, my dear,
as you came through the wood?"

"Yes, I did," said Alice:
"several thousand,
I should think."

"Four thousand
two hundred and seven,
that's the exact number,"
the King said,
referring to his book.
"I couldn't send all the horses,
you know,
because two of them a
re wanted in the game.
And I haven't sent
the two Messengers, either.
They're both gone to the town.
Just look along the road,
and tell me
if you can see either of them."

"I see nobody on the road,"
said Alice.

"I only wish I had such eyes,"
the King remarked
in a fretful tone.
"To be able to see Nobody!
And at that distance, too! Why,
it's as much as I can do
to see real people, by this light!"

All this was lost on Alice,
who was still looking intently
along the road,
shading her eyes with one hand.

"I see somebody now!"
she exclaimed at last.
"But he's coming very slowly —
and what curious attitudes
he goes into!"
(For the messenger
kept skipping up and down,
and wriggling like an eel,
as he came along,
with his great hands spread out
like fans on each side.)

"Not at all," said the King. "He's
an Anglo-Saxon Messenger —
and those
are Anglo-Saxon attitudes.
He only does them
when he's happy.
His name is Haigha."
(He pronounced it
so as to rhyme with "mayor.")

"I love my love with an H,"
Alice couldn't help beginning,
"because he is Happy.
I hate him with an H,
because he is Hideous.
I fed him with — with — with
Ham-sandwiches and Hay.
His name is Haigha,
and he lives —"

"He lives on the Hill,"
the King remarked simply,
without the least idea
that he was joining in the game,
while Alice was still hesitating
for the name of a town
beginning with H.
"The other Messenger's
called Hatta. I must have two,
you know — to come and go.
One to come, and one to go."

"I beg your pardon?" said Alice.

"It isn't respectable to beg,"
said the King.

"I only meant
that I didn't understand,"
said Alice.
"Why one to come
and one to go?"

"Didn't I tell you?"
the King repeated impatiently.
"I must have two —
to fetch and carry.
One to fetch, and one to carry."

At this moment
the Messenger arrived:
he was far too much out of breath
to say a word, and could only
wave his hands about,
and make the most fearful faces
at the poor King.

"This young lady loves you
with an H," the King said,
introducing Alice
in the hope of turning off
the Messenger's attention
from himself —
but it was no use —
the Anglo-Saxon attitudes
only got more extraordinary
every moment,
while the great eyes
rolled wildly from side to side.

"You alarm me!" said the King.
"I feel faint —
Give me a ham sandwich!"

On which the Messenger,
to Alice's great amusement,

opened a bag
that hung round his neck,
and handed a sandwich
to the King,
who devoured it greedily.

"Another sandwich!"
said the King.

"There's nothing
but hay left now,"
the Messenger said,
peeping into the bag.

"Hay, then," the King murmured
in a faint whisper.

Alice was glad to see
that it revived him a good deal.
"There's nothing like
eating hay when you're faint,"
he remarked to her,
as he munched away.

"I should think throwing
cold water over you
would be better,"
Alice suggested:
"or some sal-volatile."

"I didn't say
there was nothing better,"
the King replied.
"I said there was nothing like it."
Which Alice
did not venture to deny.

"Who did you pass on the road?"
the King went on,
holding out his hand
to the Messenger
for some more hay.

"Nobody," said the Messenger.

"Quite right," said the King:
"this young lady saw him too.
So of course
Nobody walks slower than you."

"I do my best,"
the Messenger said
in a sulky tone.
"I'm sure nobody walks
much faster than I do!"

"He can't do that," said the King,
"or else he'd have been here first.
However,
now you've got your breath,
you may tell us
what's happened in the town."

"I'll whisper it,"
said the Messenger,
putting his hands to his mouth
in the shape of a trumpet,
and stooping so as to get close
to the King's ear.
Alice was sorry for this,
as she wanted
to hear the news too.
However, instead of whispering,
he simply shouted
at the top of his voice
"They're at it again!"

"Do you call that a whisper?"
cried the poor King,
jumping up and shaking himself.
"If you do such a thing again,
I'll have you buttered!
It went through and through
my head like an earthquake!"

"It would have to be
a very tiny earthquake!"
thought Alice.

"Who are at it again?"
she ventured to ask.

"Why the Lion and the Unicorn,
of course," said the King.

"Fighting for the crown?"

"Yes, to be sure," said the King:
"and the best of the joke is,
that it's my crown all the while!
Let's run and see them."
And they trotted off,
Alice repeating to herself,
as she ran,
the words of the old song:—

"The Lion and the Unicorn
were fighting for the crown:
The Lion beat the Unicorn
all round the town.
Some gave them white bread,
some gave them brown;
Some gave them plum-cake
and drummed them out of town."

"Does—the one—that wins—
get the crown?" she asked,
as well as she could,
for the run was putting her
quite out of breath.

"Dear me, no!" said the King.
"What an idea!"

"Would you—be good enough,"
Alice panted out,
after running a little further,
"to stop a minute—just to get—
one's breath again?"

"I'm good enough,"
the King said,
"only I'm not strong enough.

You see, a minute goes by
so fearfully quick.
You might as well try
to stop a Bandersnatch!"

Alice had no more breath
for talking,
so they trotted on in silence,
till they came in sight
of a great crowd,
in the middle of which
the Lion and Unicorn
were fighting.
They were in such
a cloud of dust,
that at first Alice
could not make out
which was which:
but she soon managed
to distinguish
the Unicorn by his horn.

They placed themselves
close to where Hatta,
the other messenger,
was standing watching the fight,
with a cup of tea in one hand
and a piece of bread-and-butter
in the other.

"He's only just out of prison,
and he hadn't finished his tea
when he was sent in,"
Haigha whispered to Alice:
"and they only give them
oyster-shells in there—
so you see he's very hungry
and thirsty.
How are you, dear child?"
he went on, putting his arm
affectionately round Hatta's neck.

Hatta looked round and nodded,
and went on

with his bread and butter.

"Were you happy in prison,
dear child?" said Haigha.

Hatta looked round once more,
and this time a tear or two
trickled down his cheek:
but not a word would he say.

"Speak, can't you!"
Haigha cried impatiently.
But Hatta only munched away,
and drank some more tea.

"Speak, won't you!"
cried the King.
"How are they getting on
with the fight?"

Hatta made a desperate effort,
and swallowed a large piece
of bread-and-butter.
"They're getting on very well,"
he said in a choking voice:
"each of them has been down
about eighty-seven times."

"Then I suppose
they'll soon bring
the white bread and the brown?"
Alice ventured to remark.

"It's waiting for "em now,"
said Hatta:
"this is a bit of it as I'm eating."

There was a pause in the fight
just then,
and the Lion and the Unicorn
sat down, panting,
while the King called out
"Ten minutes allowed
for refreshments!"

Haigha and Hatta
set to work at once,
carrying rough trays
of white and brown bread.
Alice took a piece to taste,
but it was very dry.

"I don't think they'll fight
any more to-day,"
the King said to Hatta:
"go and order
the drums to begin."
And Hatta went bounding away
like a grasshopper.

For a minute or two
Alice stood silent, watching him.
Suddenly she brightened up.
"Look, look!" she cried,
pointing eagerly.
"There's the White Queen
running across the country!
She came flying out of the wood
over yonder—
How fast those Queens can run!"

"There's some enemy after her,
no doubt," the King said,
without even looking round.
"That wood's full of them."

"But aren't you going
to run and help her?" Alice asked,
very much surprised
at his taking it so quietly.

"No use, no use!" said the King.
"She runs so fearfully quick.
You might as well try
to catch a Bandersnatch!
But I'll make
a memorandum about her,
if you like—
She's a dear good creature,"

he repeated softly to himself,
as he opened
his memorandum-book.
"Do you spell 'creature'
with a double 'e'?"

At this moment the Unicorn
sauntered by them,
with his hands in his pockets.
"I had the best of it this time?"
he said to the King,
just glancing at him as he passed.

"A little—a little,"
the King replied,
rather nervously.
"You shouldn't
have run him through
with your horn, you know."

"It didn't hurt him,"
the Unicorn said carelessly,
and he was going on,
when his eye happened
to fall upon Alice:
he turned round rather instantly,
and stood for some time
looking at her
with an air of the deepest disgust.

"What—is—this?" he said at last.

"This is a child!"
Haigha replied eagerly,
coming in front of Alice
to introduce her,
and spreading out both his hands
towards her
in an Anglo-Saxon attitude.
"We only found it to-day.
It's as large as life,
and twice as natural!"

"I always thought

they were fabulous monsters!"
said the Unicorn. "Is it alive?"

"It can talk,"
said Haigha, solemnly.

The Unicorn looked dreamily
at Alice, and said "Talk, child."

Alice could not help
her lips curling up
into a smile as she began:
"Do you know,
I always thought Unicorns
were fabulous monsters, too!
I never saw one alive before!"

"Well,
now that we have seen each
other," said the Unicorn,
"if you'll believe in me,
I'll believe in you.
Is that a bargain?"

"Yes, if you like, " said Alice.

"Come, fetch out the plum-cake,
old man!" the Unicorn went on,
turning from her to the King.
"None of your brown bread
for me!"

"Certainly—certainly!"
the King muttered,
and beckoned to Haigha.
"Open the bag!" he whispered.
"Quick!
Not that one—that's full of hay!"

Haigha took a large cake
out of the bag,
and gave it to Alice to hold,
while he got out a dish
and carving-knife.

How they all came out of it
Alice couldn't guess.
It was just like a conjuring-trick,
she thought.

The Lion had joined them
while this was going on:
he looked very tired and sleepy,
and his eyes were half shut.
"What's this!" he said,
blinking lazily at Alice,
and speaking
in a deep hollow tone
that sounded like the tolling
of a great bell.

"Ah, what is it, now?"
the Unicorn cried eagerly.
"You'll never guess! I couldn't."

The Lion looked at Alice wearily.
"Are you animal—vegetable—
or mineral?" he said,
yawning at every other word.

"It's a fabulous monster!"
the Unicorn cried out,
before Alice could reply.

"Then hand round
the plum-cake, Monster,"
the Lion said, lying down
and putting his chin on his paws.
"And sit down, both of you,"
(to the King and the Unicorn):
"fair play with the cake,
you know!"

The King was evidently
very uncomfortable
at having to sit down
between the two great creatures;
but there was
no other place for him.

"What a fight
we might have for the crown,
now!" the Unicorn said,
looking slyly up at the crown,
which the poor King
was nearly shaking off his head,
he trembled so much.

"I should win easy,"
said the Lion.

"I'm not so sure of that,"
said the Unicorn.

"Why,
I beat you all round the town,
you chicken!"
the Lion replied angrily,
half getting up as he spoke.

Here the King interrupted,
to prevent the quarrel going on:
he was very nervous,
and his voice quite quivered.
"All round the town?" he said.
"That's a good long way.
Did you go by the old bridge,
or the market-place?
You get the best view
by the old bridge."

"I'm sure I don't know,"
the Lion growled out
as he lay down again.
"There was too much dust
to see anything.
What a time the Monster is,
cutting up that cake!"

Alice had seated herself
on the bank of a little brook,
with the great dish on her knees,
and was sawing away

diligently with the knife.
"It's very provoking!" she said,
in reply to the Lion
(she was getting quite used to
being called "the Monster").
"I've cut several slices already,
but they always join on again!"

"You don't know how to manage
Looking-glass cakes,"
the Unicorn remarked.
"Hand it round first,
and cut it afterwards."

This sounded nonsense,
but Alice very obediently got up,
and carried the dish round,
and the cake divided itself
into three pieces as she did so.
"Now cut it up," said the Lion,
as she returned to her place
with the empty dish.

"I say, this isn't fair!"
cried the Unicorn,
as Alice sat
with the knife in her hand,
very much puzzled how to begin.
"The Monster has given the Lion
twice as much as me!"

"She's kept none for herself,
anyhow," said the Lion.
"Do you like plum-cake,
Monster?"

But before Alice
could answer him,
the drums began.

Where the noise came from,
she couldn't make out:
the air seemed full of it,
and it rang through and through

her head
till she felt quite deafened.
She started to her feet
and sprang across the little brook
in her terror,
and had just time to see the Lion
and the Unicorn rise to their feet,
with angry looks
at being interrupted in their feast,
before she dropped to her knees,
and put her hands over her ears,
vainly trying
to shut out the dreadful uproar.

"If that doesn't
'drum them out of town,' "
 she thought to herself,
"nothing ever will!"

CHAPTER VIII.

"It's my own Invention"

After a while the noise
seemed gradually to die away,
till all was dead silence,
and Alice lifted up her head
in some alarm.
There was no one to be seen,
and her first thought
was that she must have been
dreaming about the Lion
and the Unicorn
and those queer
Anglo-Saxon Messengers.
However,
there was the great dish
still lying at her feet,
on which she had tried
to cut the plum-cake,
"So I wasn't dreaming, after all,"
she said to herself,
"unless—unless we're all part
of the same dream.
Only I do hope it's my dream,
and not the Red King's!
I don't like belonging
to another person's dream,"
she went on
in a rather complaining tone:
"I've a great mind
to go and wake him,
and see what happens!"

At this moment her thoughts
were interrupted
by a loud shouting of "Ahoy!
Ahoy! Check!"
and a Knight dressed
in crimson armour
came galloping down upon her,
brandishing a great club.
Just as he reached her,
the horse stopped suddenly:
"You're my prisoner!"
the Knight cried,
as he tumbled off his horse.

Startled as she was, Alice
was more frightened for him
than for herself at the moment,
and watched him
with some anxiety
as he mounted again.
As soon as he was comfortably
in the saddle,
he began once more
"You're my—"
but here another voice broke in
"Ahoy! Ahoy! Check!"
and Alice looked round
in some surprise
for the new enemy.

This time it was a White Knight.
He drew up at Alice's side,
and tumbled off his horse
just as the Red Knight had done:
then he got on again,
and the two Knights
sat and looked at each other
for some time without speaking.
Alice looked from one
to the other
in some bewilderment.

"She's my prisoner, you know!"
the Red Knight said at last.

"Yes,
but then I came and rescued her!"
the White Knight replied.

"Well, we must fight for her,
then," said the Red Knight,
as he took up his helmet
(which hung from the saddle,

and was something
the shape of a horse's head),
and put it on.

"You will observe
the Rules of Battle, of course?"
the White Knight remarked,
putting on his helmet too.

"I always do,"
said the Red Knight,
and they began banging away
at each other with such fury
that Alice got behind a tree
to be out of the way of the blows.

"I wonder, now,
what the Rules of Battle are,"
she said to herself,
as she watched the fight,
timidly peeping out
from her hiding-place:
"one Rule seems to be,
that if one Knight hits the other,
he knocks him off his horse,
and if he misses,
he tumbles off himself—
and another Rule seems to be
that they hold their clubs
with their arms,
as if they were Punch and Judy—
What a noise
they make when they tumble!
Just like a whole set of fire-irons
falling into the fender!
And how quiet the horses are!
They let them get on and off them
just as if they were tables!"

Another Rule of Battle,
that Alice had not noticed,
seemed to be that they
always fell on their heads,
and the battle ended

with their both
falling off in this way,
side by side:
when they got up again,
they shook hands,
and then the Red Knight
mounted and galloped off.

"It was a glorious victory,
wasn't it?" said the White Knight,
as he came up panting.

"I don't know,"
Alice said doubtfully.
"I don't want to be
anybody's prisoner.
I want to be a Queen."

"So you will,
when you've crossed
the next brook,"
said the White Knight.
"I'll see you safe to the end
of the wood—
and then I must go back,
you know.
That's the end of my move."

"Thank you very much,"
said Alice.
"May I help you off
with your helmet?"
It was evidently more than he
could manage by himself;
however,
she managed to shake him
out of it at last.

"Now one can breathe
more easily," said the Knight,
putting back his shaggy hair
with both hands,
and turning his gentle face
and large mild eyes to Alice.

She thought she had never seen
such a strange-looking soldier
in all her life.

He was dressed in tin armour,
which seemed to fit him
very badly,
and he had a queer-shaped
little deal box fastened
across his shoulder,
upside-down,
and with the lid hanging open.
Alice looked
at it with great curiosity.

"I see you're admiring
my little box."
the Knight said in a friendly tone.
"It's my own invention—
to keep clothes
and sandwiches in.
You see I carry it upside-down,
so that the rain can't get in."

"But the things can get out,"
Alice gently remarked.
"Do you know the lid's open?"

"I didn't know it,"
the Knight said,
a shade of vexation
passing over his face.
"Then all the things
must have fallen out!
And the box
is no use without them."
He unfastened it as he spoke,
and was just going
to throw it into the bushes,
when a sudden thought
seemed to strike him,
and he hung it carefully on a tree.
"Can you guess why I did that?"
he said to Alice.

Alice shook her head.

"In hopes some bees
may make a nest in it—
then I should get the honey."

"But you've got a bee-hive—
or something like one—
fastened to the saddle,"
said Alice.

"Yes, it's a very good bee-hive,"
the Knight
 said in a discontented tone,
"one of the best kind.
But not a single bee
has come near it yet.
And the other thing
is a mouse-trap.
I suppose the mice
keep the bees out—
or the bees keep the mice out,
I don't know which."

"I was wondering
what the mouse-trap was for,"
said Alice.
"It isn't very likely there would
be any mice on the horse's back."

"Not very likely, perhaps,"
said the Knight:
"but if they do come,
I don't choose to have them
running all about."

"You see,"
he went on after a pause,
"it's as well to be
provided for everything .
That's the reason the horse
has all those anklets
round his feet."

"But what are they for?"
Alice asked
in a tone of great curiosity.

"To guard against the bites
of sharks," the Knight replied.
"It's an invention of my own.
And now help me on.
I'll go with you to the end
of the wood —
What's the dish for?"

"It's meant for plum-cake,"
said Alice.

"We'd better take it with us,"
the Knight said.
"It'll come in handy
if we find any plum-cake.
Help me to get it into this bag."

This took a very long time
to manage,
though Alice held the bag open
very carefully,
because the Knight
was so very awkward
in putting in the dish:
the first two or three times
that he tried
he fell in himself instead.
"It's rather a tight fit, you see,"
he said, as they got it in a last;
"There are so many candlesticks
in the bag."
And he hung it to the saddle,
which was already loaded
with bunches of carrots,
and fire-irons,
and many other things.

"I hope you've got your hair
well fastened on?" he continued,

as they set off.

"Only in the usual way,"
Alice said, smiling.

"That's hardly enough,"
he said, anxiously.
"You see the wind
is so very strong here.
It's as strong as soup."

"Have you invented a plan
for keeping the hair
from being blown off?"
Alice enquired.

"Not yet," said the Knight.
"But I've got a plan
for keeping it from falling off."

"I should like to hear it,
very much."

"First you take an upright stick,"
said the Knight.
"Then you make your hair
creep up it, like a fruit-tree.
Now the reason hair falls off
is because it hangs down —
things never fall upwards,
you know.
It's a plan of my own invention.
You may try it if you like."

It didn't sound
a comfortable plan,
Alice thought,
and for a few minutes
she walked on in silence,
puzzling over the idea,
and every now and then
stopping to help the poor Knight,
who certainly
was not a good rider.

Whenever the horse stopped
(which it did very often),
he fell off in front;
and whenever it went on again
(which it generally did
rather suddenly),
he fell off behind.
Otherwise he kept on pretty well,
except that he had a habit
of now and then
falling off sideways;
and as he generally did
this on the side
on which Alice was walking,
she soon found that it
was the best plan not to walk
quite close to the horse.

"I'm afraid you've not had
much practice in riding,"
she ventured to say,
as she was helping him up
from his fifth tumble.

The Knight
looked very much surprised,
and a little offended
at the remark.
"What makes you say that?"
he asked,
as he scrambled back
into the saddle,
keeping hold of Alice's hair
with one hand,
to save himself from falling over
on the other side.

"Because people
don't fall off quite so often,
when they've had
much practice."

"I've had plenty of practice,"
the Knight said very gravely:
"plenty of practice!"

Alice could think
of nothing better to say than
"Indeed?" but she said it
as heartily as she could.
They went on a little way
in silence after this,
the Knight with his eyes shut,
muttering to himself,
and Alice watching anxiously
for the next tumble.

"The great art of riding,"
the Knight
suddenly began in a loud voice,
waving his right arm as he spoke,
"is to keep—"
Here the sentence ended
as suddenly as it had begun,
as the Knight fell heavily
on the top of his head
exactly in the path
where Alice was walking.
She was quite frightened
this time,
and said in an anxious tone,
as she picked him up,
"I hope no bones are broken?"

"None to speak of,"
the Knight said,
as if he didn't mind
breaking two or three of them.
"The great art of riding,
as I was saying, is—
to keep your balance properly.
Like this, you know—"

He let go the bridle,
and stretched out both his arms
to show Alice what he meant,
and this time he fell flat

on his back,
right under the horse's feet.

"Plenty of practice!"
he went on repeating,
all the time that Alice
was getting him on his feet again.
"Plenty of practice!"

"It's too ridiculous!" cried Alice,
losing all her patience this time.
"You ought to have
a wooden horse on wheels,
that you ought!"

"Does that kind go smoothly?"
the Knight asked
in a tone of great interest,
clasping his arms round
the horse's neck as he spoke,
just in time to save himself
from tumbling off again.

"Much more smoothly
than a live horse," Alice said,
with a little scream of laughter,
in spite of all she could do
to prevent it.

"I'll get one," the Knight said
thoughtfully to himself.
"One or two—several."

There was a short silence
after this, and then the Knight
went on again. "I'm a great hand
at inventing things.
Now, I daresay you noticed,
that last time you picked me up,
that I was looking
rather thoughtful?"

"You were a little grave,"
said Alice.

"Well, just then
I was inventing a new way
of getting over a gate—
would you like to hear it?"

"Very much indeed,"
Alice said politely.

"I'll tell you how
I came to think of it,"
said the Knight. "You see,
I said to myself,
'The only difficulty
is with the feet:
the head is high enough already.'
Now, first I put my head
on the top of the gate—
then I stand on my head—
then the feet are high enough,
you see—then I'm over, you see."

"Yes, I suppose you'd be over
when that was done,"
Alice said thoughtfully:
"but don't you think
it would be rather hard?"

"I haven't tried it yet,"
the Knight said, gravely:
"so I can't tell for certain—
but I'm afraid it would be
a little hard."

He looked so vexed at the idea,
that Alice
changed the subject hastily.
"What a curious helmet
you've got!" she said cheerfully.
"Is that your invention too?"

The Knight looked down
proudly at his helmet,
which hung from the saddle.

"Yes, " he said,
"but I've invented
a better one than that—
like a sugar loaf.
When I used to wear it,
if I fell off the horse,
it always touched
the ground directly.
So I had a very little way to fall,
you see—
But there was the danger
of falling into it, to be sure.
That happened to me once—
and the worst of it was,
before I could get out again,
the other White Knight
came and put it on.
He thought
it was his own helmet."

The knight looked so solemn
about it that Alice
did not dare to laugh.
"I'm afraid
you must have hurt him,"
she said in a trembling voice,
"being on the top of his head."

"I had to kick him, of course,"
the Knight said, very seriously.
"And then he took
the helmet off again—
but it took hours and hours
to get me out.
I was as fast as—as lightning,
you know."

"But that's a different kind
of fastness," Alice objected.

The Knight shook his head.
"It was all kinds
of fastness with me,
I can assure you!" he said.

He raised his hands
in some excitement
as he said this,
and instantly rolled out
of the saddle,
and fell headlong
into a deep ditch.

Alice ran to the side
of the ditch to look for him.
She was rather startled by the fall,
as for some time
he had kept on very well,
and she was afraid
that he really was hurt this time.
However,
though she could see nothing
but the soles of his feet,
she was much relieved
to hear that he was talking
on in his usual tone.
"All kinds of fastness,"
he repeated:
"but it was careless of him
to put another man's helmet on
—with the man in it, too."

"How can you go on talking
so quietly, head downwards?"
Alice asked,
as she dragged him out
by the feet,
and laid him in a heap
on the bank.

The Knight looked surprised
at the question.
"What does it matter
where my body happens to be?"
he said.
"My mind goes on working
all the same. In fact,
the more head downwards I am,
the more I keep inventing

new things."

"Now the cleverest thing
of the sort that I ever did,"
he went on after a pause,
"was inventing a new pudding
during the meat-course."

"In time to have it cooked
for the next course?" said Alice.
"Well, not the next course,"
the Knight said
in a slow thoughtful tone: "no,
certainly not the next course ."

"Then it would have to be
the next day.
I suppose you wouldn't have
two pudding-courses
in one dinner?"

"Well, not the next day,"
the Knight repeated as before:
"not the next day . In fact,"
he went on,
holding his head down,
and his voice
getting lower and lower,
"I don't believe
that pudding ever was cooked!
In fact,
I don't believe
that pudding ever will be cooked!
And yet it was
a very clever pudding to invent."

"What did you mean
it to be made of?" Alice asked,
hoping to cheer him up,
for the poor Knight seemed
quite low-spirited about it.

"It began with blotting paper,"
the Knight

answered with a groan.

"That wouldn't be very nice,
I'm afraid—"

"Not very nice alone,"
he interrupted, quite eagerly:
"but you've no idea
what a difference it makes
mixing it with other things—
such as gunpowder
and sealing-wax.
And here I must leave you."
They had just come
to the end of the wood.

Alice could only look puzzled:
she was thinking of the pudding.

"You are sad,"
the Knight said
in an anxious tone:
"let me sing you a song
to comfort you."

"Is it very long?" Alice asked,
for she had heard a good deal
of poetry that day.

"It's long," said the Knight,
"but very, very beautiful.
Everybody
that hears me sing it—
either it brings the tears
into their eyes, or else—"

"Or else what?" said Alice,
for the Knight
had made a sudden pause.

"Or else it doesn't, you know.
The name of the song is called
' Haddocks' Eyes .' "

"Oh, that's the name of the song,
is it?" Alice said,
trying to feel interested.

"No, you don't understand,"
the Knight said,
looking a little vexed.
"That's what the name is called.
The name really is
' The Aged Aged Man. ' "

"Then I ought to have said
'That's what the song is called'?"
Alice corrected herself.

"No, you oughtn't:
that's quite another thing!
The song is called
' Ways and Means ':
but that's only what it's called,
you know!"

"Well, what is the song, then?"
said Alice,
who was by this time
completely bewildered.

"I was coming to that,"
the Knight said.
"The song really is
' A-sitting On A Gate ':
and the tune's
my own invention."

So saying,
he stopped his horse
and let the reins fall on its neck:
then, slowly beating time
with one hand,
and with a faint smile
lighting up his gentle foolish face,
as if he enjoyed the music
of his song, he began.

Of all the strange things
that Alice saw in her journey
Through The Looking-Glass,
this was the one
that she always remembered
most clearly.
Years afterwards she could bring
the whole scene back again,
as if it had been only yesterday—
the mild blue eyes
and kindly smile of the Knight—
the setting sun
gleaming through his hair,
and shining on his armour
in a blaze of light
that quite dazzled her—
the horse quietly moving about,
with the reins hanging loose
on his neck,
cropping the grass at her feet—
and the black shadows
of the forest behind—
all this she took in like a picture,
as,
with one hand shading her eyes,
she leant against a tree,
watching the strange pair,
and listening, in a half dream,
to the melancholy music
of the song.

"But the tune
isn't his own invention,"
she said to herself:
"it's ' I give thee all,
I can no more.' "
She stood and listened
very attentively,
but no tears came into her eyes.

"I'll tell thee everything I can;

There's little to relate.
I saw an aged aged man,

A-sitting on a gate.

'Who are you, aged man?' I said,

'and how is it you live?'
And his answer trickled
through my head
Like water through a sieve.

He said 'I look for butterflies
That sleep among the wheat:

I make them into mutton-pies,

And sell them in the street.

I sell them unto men,' he said,

'Who sail on stormy seas;

And that's the way
I get my bread—
A trifle, if you please.'

But I was thinking of a plan
To dye one's whiskers green,

And always use so large a fan
That they could not be seen.

So,
having no reply to give
To what the old man said,

I cried, 'Come,
tell me how you live!'
And thumped him on the head.

His accents mild took up the tale:

He said 'I go my ways,

And when I find a mountain-rill,

I set it in a blaze;

And thence they make
a stuff they call
Rolands' Macassar Oil—
Yet twopence-halfpenny is all
They give me for my toil.'

But I was thinking of a way
To feed oneself on batter,

And so go on from day to day
Getting a little fatter.

I shook him well
from side to side,

Until his face was blue:

'Come,
tell me how you live,' I cried,

'And what it is you do!'

He said 'I hunt
for haddocks' eyes
Among the heather bright,

And work them
into waistcoat-buttons
In the silent night.

And these I do not sell for gold
Or coin of silvery shine
But for a copper halfpenny,

And that will purchase nine.

'I sometimes dig
for buttered rolls,

Or set limed twigs for crabs;

I sometimes search
the grassy knolls
 For wheels of Hansom-cabs.

And that's the way'
(he gave a wink)
 'By which I get my wealth—
And very gladly will I drink
 Your Honour's noble health.'

I heard him then, for I had just
 Completed my design
To keep the Menai bridge
from rust
 By boiling it in wine.

I thanked him much
 for telling me
The way he got his wealth,

But chiefly for his wish that he
 Might drink my noble health.

And now,
if e'er by chance I put
 My fingers into glue
Or madly squeeze
a right-hand foot
 Into a left-hand shoe,

Or if I drop upon my toe
 A very heavy weight,

I weep, for it reminds me so,

Of that old man I used to know—
Whose look was mild,
whose speech was slow,

Whose hair was whiter
than the snow,

Whose face was very like a crow,

With eyes, like cinders, all aglow,

Who seemed distracted
with his woe,

Who rocked his body to and fro,

And muttered mumblingly
and low,

As if his mouth
were full of dough,

Who snorted like a buffalo—
That summer evening, long ago,

 A-sitting on a gate."

As the Knight
sang the last words of the ballad,
he gathered up the reins,
and turned his horse's head
along the road
by which they had come.
"You've only a few yards to go,"
he said,
"down the hill
and over that little brook,
and then you'll be a Queen—
But you'll stay
and see me off first?"
he added as Alice turned
with an eager look
in the direction
to which he pointed.
"I shan't be long. You'll wait
and wave your handkerchief
when I get to that turn
in the road?
I think it'll encourage me,
you see."

"Of course I'll wait," said Alice:
"and thank you very much

for coming so far—
and for the song—
I liked it very much."

"I hope so,"
the Knight said doubtfully:
"but you didn't cry so much
as I thought you would."

So they shook hands,
and then the Knight
rode slowly away into the forest.
"It won't take long to see him off,
I expect," Alice said to herself,
as she stood watching him.
"There he goes!
Right on his head as usual!
However,
he gets on again pretty easily—
that comes of having
so many things
hung round the horse—"
So she went on talking to herself,
as she watched the horse
walking leisurely along the road,
and the Knight tumbling off,
first on one side
and then on the other.
After the fourth or fifth tumble
he reached the turn,
and then she waved
her handkerchief to him,
and waited
till he was out of sight.

"I hope it encouraged him,"
she said, as she turned
to run down the hill:
"and now for the last brook,
and to be a Queen!
How grand it sounds!"
A very few steps brought her
to the edge of the brook.
"The Eighth Square at last!"

she cried as she bounded across,
and threw herself down to rest
on a lawn as soft as moss,
with little flower-beds
dotted about it here and there.
"Oh, how glad I am to get here!
And what is this on my head?"
she exclaimed
in a tone of dismay,
as she put her hands up
to something very heavy,
and fitted tight
all round her head.

"But how can it have got there
without my knowing it?"
she said to herself,
as she lifted it off,
and set it on her lap to make out
what it could possibly be.

It was a golden crown.

CHAPTER IX.

Queen Alice

"Well, this is grand!" said Alice.
"I never expected I should be
a Queen so soon—
and I'll tell you what it is,
your majesty,"
she went on in a severe tone
(she was always rather fond of
scolding herself),
"it'll never do for you
to be lolling about
on the grass like that!
Queens have to be dignified,
you know!"

So she got up and walked about
—rather stiffly just at first,
as she was afraid
that the crown might come off:
but she comforted herself
with the thought that there was
nobody to see her,
"and if I really am a Queen,"
she said as she sat down again,
"I shall be able
to manage it quite well in time."

Everything was happening
so oddly that she didn't feel
a bit surprised at finding
the Red Queen
and the White Queen
sitting close to her,
one on each side:
she would have liked
very much to ask them
how they came there,
but she feared
it would not be quite civil.
However,
there would be no harm,
she thought,
in asking if the game was over.
"Please, would you tell me—"
she began,
looking timidly at the Red Queen.

"Speak when you're spoken to!"
The Queen
sharply interrupted her.

"But if everybody
obeyed that rule," said Alice,
who was always ready
for a little argument,
"and if you only spoke
when you were spoken to,
and the other person
always waited for you to begin,
you see nobody
would ever say anything,
so that—"

"Ridiculous!" cried the Queen.
"Why, don't you see, child—"
here she broke off with a frown,
and, after thinking for a minute,
suddenly changed the subject
of the conversation.
"What do you mean by
'If you really are a Queen'?
What right have you
to call yourself so?
You can't be a Queen, you know,
till you've passed
the proper examination.
And the sooner we begin it,
the better."

"I only said 'if'!"
poor Alice pleaded
in a piteous tone.

The two Queens
looked at each other,

and the Red Queen remarked,
with a little shudder,
"She says she only said 'if'—"

"But she said a great deal more
than that!"
the White Queen moaned,
wringing her hands. "Oh,
ever so much more than that!"

"So you did, you know,"
the Red Queen said to Alice.
"Always speak the truth—
think before you speak—
and write it down afterwards."

"I'm sure I didn't mean—"
Alice was beginning,
but the Red Queen
interrupted her impatiently.

"That's just what I complain of!
You should have meant!
What do you suppose is the use
of child without any meaning?
Even a joke
should have some meaning—
and a child's
more important than a joke,
I hope. You couldn't deny that,
even if you tried
with both hands."

"I don't deny things
with my hands," Alice objected.

"Nobody said you did,"
said the Red Queen.
"I said you couldn't if you tried."

"She's in that state of mind,"
said the White Queen,
"that she wants
to deny something —

only she doesn't know
what to deny!"

"A nasty, vicious temper,"
the Red Queen remarked;
and then there was
an uncomfortable silence
for a minute or two.

The Red Queen broke the silence
by saying to the White Queen,
"I invite you to Alice's
dinner-party this afternoon."

The White Queen smiled feebly,
and said "And I invite you."

"I didn't know
I was to have a party at all,"
said Alice;
"but if there is to be one,
I think I ought
to invite the guests."

"We gave you
the opportunity of doing it,"
the Red Queen remarked:
"but I daresay you've not had
many lessons in manners yet?"

"Manners are not taught
in lessons," said Alice.
"Lessons teach you to do sums,
and things of that sort."

"And you do Addition?"
the White Queen asked.
"What's one and one and one
and one and one and one
and one and one and one
and one?"

"I don't know," said Alice.
"I lost count."

"She can't do Addition,"
the Red Queen interrupted.
"Can you do Subtraction?
Take nine from eight."

"Nine from eight I can't,
you know,"
Alice replied very readily:
"but—"

"She can't do Subtraction,"
said the White Queen.
"Can you do Division?
Divide a loaf by a knife—
what's the answer to that?"

"I suppose—"
Alice was beginning,
but the Red Queen
answered for her.
"Bread-and-butter, of course.
Try another Subtraction sum.
Take a bone from a dog:
what remains?"

Alice considered.
"The bone wouldn't remain,
of course, if I took it—
and the dog wouldn't remain;
it would come to bite me—
and I'm sure I shouldn't remain!"

"Then you think
nothing would remain?"
said the Red Queen.

"I think that's the answer."

"Wrong, as usual,"
said the Red Queen:
"the dog's temper
would remain."

"But I don't see how—"

"Why, look here!"
the Red Queen cried.
"The dog would lose its temper,
wouldn't it?"

"Perhaps it would,"
Alice replied cautiously.

"Then if the dog went away,
its temper would remain!"
the Queen exclaimed
triumphantly.

Alice said,
as gravely as she could,
"They might go different ways."
But she couldn't help
thinking to herself,
"What dreadful nonsense
we are talking!"

"She can't do sums a bit !"
the Queens said together,
with great emphasis.

"Can you do sums?" Alice said,
turning suddenly
on the White Queen,
for she didn't like
being found fault with so much.

The Queen gasped
and shut her eyes.
"I can do Addition,
if you give me time—
but I can't do Subtraction,
under any circumstances!"

"Of course you know
your A B C?" said the Red Queen.

"To be sure I do." said Alice.

"So do I,"
the White Queen whispered:
"we'll often say it over together,
dear. And I'll tell you a secret—
I can read words of one letter!
Isn't that grand! However,
don't be discouraged.
You'll come to it in time."

Here the Red Queen began again.
"Can you answer
useful questions?" she said.
"How is bread made?"

"I know that !"
Alice cried eagerly.
"You take some flour—"

"Where do you pick the flower?"
the White Queen asked.
"In a garden, or in the hedges?"

"Well, it isn't picked at all,"
Alice explained: "it's ground —"

"How many acres of ground?"
said the White Queen.
"You mustn't leave out
so many things."

"Fan her head!" the Red Queen
anxiously interrupted.
"She'll be feverish
after so much thinking."
So they set to work
and fanned her
with bunches of leaves,
till she had to beg them
to leave off,
it blew her hair about so.

"She's all right again now,"
said the Red Queen.

"Do you know Languages?
What's the French
for fiddle-de-dee?"

"Fiddle-de-dee's not English,"
Alice replied gravely.

"Who ever said it was?"
said the Red Queen.

Alice thought she saw a way
out of the difficulty this time.
"If you'll tell me what language
'fiddle-de-dee' is,
I'll tell you the French for it!"
she exclaimed triumphantly.

But the Red Queen
drew herself up rather stiffly,
and said
"Queens never make bargains."

"I wish Queens
never asked questions,"
Alice thought to herself.

"Don't let us quarrel,"
the White Queen said
in an anxious tone.
"What is the cause of lightning?"

"The cause of lightning,"
Alice said very decidedly,
for she felt quite certain
about this,
"is the thunder—no, no!"
she hastily corrected herself.
"I meant the other way."

"It's too late to correct it,"
said the Red Queen:
"when you've once said a thing,
that fixes it,
and you must take

the consequences."

"Which reminds me—"
the White Queen said,
looking down
and nervously clasping
and unclasping her hands,
"we had such a thunderstorm
last Tuesday—
I mean one of the last set
of Tuesdays, you know."

Alice was puzzled.
"In our country," she remarked,
"there's only one day at a time."

The Red Queen said,
"That's a poor thin way
of doing things. Now here,
we mostly have days and nights
two or three at a time,
and sometimes in the winter
we take as many
as five nights together—
for warmth, you know."

"Are five nights
warmer than one night, then?"
Alice ventured to ask.

"Five times as warm, of course."

"But they should be
five times as cold,
by the same rule—"

"Just so!" cried the Red Queen.
"Five times as warm,
and five times as cold—
just as I'm five times
as rich as you are,
and five times as clever!"

Alice sighed and gave it up.

"It's exactly like a riddle
with no answer!" she thought.

"Humpty Dumpty saw it too,"
the White Queen went on
in a low voice,
more as if she were
talking to herself.
"He came to the door
with a corkscrew in his hand—"

"What did he want?"
said the Red Queen.

"He said he would come in,"
the White Queen went on,
"because he was
looking for a hippopotamus.
Now, as it happened,
there wasn't such a thing
in the house, that morning."

"Is there generally?"
Alice asked in an astonished tone.

"Well, only on Thursdays,"
said the Queen.

"I know what he came for,"
said Alice:
"he wanted to punish the fish,
because—"

Here the White Queen
began again.
"It was such a thunderstorm,
you can't think!"
("She never could, you know,"
said the Red Queen.)
"And part of the roof came off,
and ever so much
thunder got in—
and it went rolling
round the room in great lumps—

and knocking over the tables
and things—
till I was so frightened,
I couldn't remember
my own name!"

Alice thought to herself,
"I never should try to remember
my name in the middle
of an accident!
Where would be the use of it?"
but she did not say this aloud,
for fear of hurting
the poor Queen's feeling.

"Your Majesty must excuse her,"
the Red Queen said to Alice,
taking one of
the White Queen's hands
in her own,
and gently stroking it:
"she means well,
but she can't help
saying foolish things,
as a general rule."

The White Queen
looked timidly at Alice,
who felt she ought
to say something kind,
but really couldn't
think of anything at the moment.

"She never was really well
brought up,"
the Red Queen went on:
"but it's amazing
how good-tempered she is!
Pat her on the head,
and see how pleased she'll be!"
But this was more than Alice
had courage to do.

"A little kindness—

and putting her hair in papers—
would do wonders with her—"

The White Queen
gave a deep sigh,
and laid her head
on Alice's shoulder.
"I am so sleepy?" she moaned.

"She's tired, poor thing!"
said the Red Queen.
"Smooth her hair—
lend her your nightcap—
and sing her a soothing lullaby."

"I haven't got a nightcap
with me," said Alice,
as she tried to obey
the first direction:
"and I don't know
any soothing lullabies."

"I must do it myself, then,"
said the Red Queen,
and she began:

"Hush-a-by lady, in Alice's lap!

Till the feast's ready,
we've time for a nap:

When the feast's over,
we'll go to the ball—
Red Queen, and White Queen,
and Alice, and all!

"And now you know the words,"
she added,
as she put her head down
on Alice's other shoulder,
"just sing it through to me .
I'm getting sleepy, too."
In another moment
both Queens were fast asleep,

and snoring loud.

"What am I to do?"
exclaimed Alice,
looking about in great perplexity,
as first one round head,
and then the other,
rolled down from her shoulder,
and lay like a heavy lump
in her lap. "I don't think
it ever happened before,
that any one had to take care of
two Queens asleep at once!
No, not in all
the History of England—
it couldn't, you know,
because there never was more
than one Queen at a time.
Do wake up, you heavy things!"
she went on in an impatient tone;
but there was no answer
but a gentle snoring.

The snoring got more distinct
every minute,
and sounded more like a tune:
at last she could even make out
the words,
and she listened so eagerly that,
when the two great heads
vanished from her lap,
she hardly missed them.

She was standing
before an arched doorway
over which were the words
QUEEN ALICE in large letters,
and on each side of the arch
there was a bell-handle;
one was marked "Visitors' Bell,"
and the other "Servants' Bell."

"I'll wait till the song's over,"
thought Alice,

"and then I'll ring—the—
which bell must I ring?"
she went on,
very much puzzled by the names.
"I'm not a visitor,
and I'm not a servant.
There ought to be one marked
'Queen,' you know—"

Just then the door
opened a little way,
and a creature with a long beak
put its head out for a moment
and said "No admittance
till the week after next!"
and shut the door again
with a bang.

Alice knocked
and rang in vain for a long time,
but at last, a very old Frog,
who was sitting under a tree,
got up and hobbled
slowly towards her:
he was dressed in bright yellow,
and had enormous boots on.

"What is it, now?" the Frog said
in a deep hoarse whisper.

Alice turned round,
ready to find fault with anybody.
"Where's the servant
whose business it is
to answer the door?"
she began angrily.

"Which door?" said the Frog.

Alice almost stamped
with irritation at the slow drawl
in which he spoke.
"This door, of course!"

The Frog looked at the door
with his large dull eyes
for a minute:
then he went nearer
and rubbed it with his thumb,
as if he were trying whether
the paint would come off;
then he looked at Alice.

"To answer the door?" he said.
"What's it been asking of?"
He was so hoarse that Alice
could scarcely hear him.

"I don't know what you mean,"
she said.

"I talks English, doesn't I?"
the Frog went on.
"Or are you deaf?
What did it ask you?"

"Nothing!"
Alice said impatiently.
"I've been knocking at it!"

"Shouldn't do that—
shouldn't do that—"
the Frog muttered.
"Vexes it, you know."
Then he went up
and gave the door a kick
with one of his great feet.
"You let it alone," he panted out,
as he hobbled back to his tree,
"and it'll let you alone,
you know."

At this moment
the door was flung open,
and a shrill voice
was heard singing:

"To the Looking-Glass

world it was Alice that said,

'I've a sceptre in hand,
I've a crown on my head;

Let the Looking-Glass creatures,
whatever they be,

Come and dine
with the Red Queen,
the White Queen, and me.' "

And hundreds of voices
joined in the chorus:

"Then fill up the glasses
as quick as you can,

And sprinkle the table
with buttons and bran:

Put cats in the coffee,
and mice in the tea—
And welcome Queen Alice
with thirty-times-three!"

Then followed
a confused noise of cheering,
and Alice thought to herself,
"Thirty times three makes ninety.
I wonder if any one's counting?"
In a minute
there was silence again,
and the same shrill
voice sang another verse;

" 'O Looking-Glass creatures,
'quoth Alice,' draw near!

"Tis an honour to see me,
a favour to hear:

"Tis a privilege high
to have dinner and tea

Along with the Red Queen,
the White Queen, and me!' "

Then came the chorus again:—

"Then fill up the glasses
with treacle and ink,

Or anything else
that is pleasant to drink:

Mix sand with the cider,
and wool with the wine—
And welcome Queen Alice
with ninety-times-nine!"

"Ninety times nine!"
Alice repeated in despair,
"Oh, that'll never be done!
I'd better go in at once—"
and there was a dead silence
the moment she appeared.

Alice glanced nervously
along the table,
as she walked up the large hall,
and noticed that there were
about fifty guests, of all kinds:
some were animals, some birds,
and there were even
a few flowers among them.
"I'm glad they've come
without waiting to be asked,"
she thought:
"I should never have known
who were the right people
to invite!"

There were three chairs
at the head of the table;
the Red and White Queens
had already taken two of them,
but the middle one was empty.
Alice sat down in it,

rather uncomfortable
in the silence, and longing
for some one to speak.

At last the Red Queen began.
"You've missed the soup
and fish," she said.
"Put on the joint!"
And the waiters set
a leg of mutton before Alice,
who looked at it rather anxiously,
as she had never had
to carve a joint before.

"You look a little shy;
let me introduce you
to that leg of mutton,"
said the Red Queen.
"Alice—Mutton; Mutton—Alice."
The leg of mutton
got up in the dish
and made a little bow to Alice;
and Alice returned the bow,
not knowing whether
to be frightened or amused.

"May I give you a slice?"
she said,
taking up the knife and fork,
and looking from
one Queen to the other.

"Certainly not,"
the Red Queen said,
very decidedly:
"it isn't etiquette to cut any one
you've been introduced to.
Remove the joint!"
And the waiters carried it off,
and brought a large
plum-pudding in its place.

"I won't be introduced
to the pudding, please,"

Alice said rather hastily,
"or we shall get no dinner at all.
May I give you some?"

But the Red Queen looked sulky,
and growled "Pudding—Alice;
Alice—Pudding.
Remove the pudding!"
and the waiters took it away
so quickly that Alice
couldn't return its bow.

However, she didn't see why
the Red Queen
should be the only one
to give orders, so,
as an experiment,
she called out "Waiter!
Bring back the pudding!"
and there it was again
in a moment
like a conjuring-trick.
It was so large
that she couldn't help feeling
a little shy with it,
as she had been with the mutton;
however,
she conquered her shyness
by a great effort and cut a slice
and handed it to the Red Queen.

"What impertinence!"
said the Pudding.
"I wonder how you'd like it,
if I were to cut a slice out of you,
you creature!"

It spoke in a thick,
suety sort of voice,
and Alice hadn't a word
to say in reply:
she could only sit
and look at it and gasp.

"Make a remark,"
said the Red Queen:
"it's ridiculous to leave
all the conversation
to the pudding!"

"Do you know,
I've had such a quantity of poetry
repeated to me to-day,"
Alice began,
a little frightened at finding that,
the moment she opened her lips,
there was dead silence,
and all eyes were fixed upon her;
"and it's a very curious thing,
I think—
every poem was about fishes
in some way.
Do you know why
they're so fond of fishes,
all about here?"

She spoke to the Red Queen,
whose answer
was a little wide of the mark.
"As to fishes," she said,
very slowly and solemnly,
putting her mouth close
to Alice's ear,
"her White Majesty
knows a lovely riddle—
all in poetry—all about fishes.
Shall she repeat it?"

"Her Red Majesty's very kind
to mention it," the White Queen
murmured into Alice's other ear,
in a voice like the cooing
of a pigeon.
"It would be such a treat! May I?"

"Please do,"
Alice said very politely.

The White Queen laughed
with delight,
and stroked Alice's cheek.
Then she began:

" 'First, the fish must be caught.'
That is easy: a baby, I think,
could have caught it.

'Next, the fish must be bought.'
That is easy: a penny, I think,
would have bought it.

'Now cook me the fish!'
That is easy, and will not take
more than a minute.

'Let it lie in a dish!'
That is easy,
because it already is in it.

'Bring it here! Let me sup!'
It is easy to set
such a dish on the table.

'Take the dish-cover up!'
Ah, that is so hard
that I fear I'm unable!

For it holds it like glue—
Holds the lid to the dish,
while it lies in the middle:

Which is easiest to do,

Un-dish-cover the fish,
or dishcover the riddle?"

"Take a minute to think about it,
and then guess,"
said the Red Queen.
"Meanwhile,
we'll drink your health—
Queen Alice's health!"

she screamed
at the top of her voice,
and all the guests
began drinking it directly,
and very queerly
they managed it: some of them
put their glasses upon their heads
like extinguishers, and drank all
that trickled down their faces—
others upset the decanters,
and drank the wine
as it ran off the edges
of the table—and three of them
(who looked like kangaroos)
scrambled into the dish
of roast mutton,
and began eagerly
lapping up the gravy,
"just like pigs in a trough!"
thought Alice.

"You ought to return thanks
in a neat speech,"
the Red Queen said,
frowning at Alice as she spoke.

"We must support you,
you know,"
the White Queen whispered,
as Alice got up to do it,
very obediently,
but a little frightened.

"Thank you very much,"
she whispered in reply,
"but I can do quite well without."

"That wouldn't be
at all the thing,"
the Red Queen said
very decidedly:
so Alice tried to submit to it
with a good grace.

("And they did push so!"
she said afterwards,
when she was telling her sister
the history of the feast.
"You would have thought
they wanted to squeeze me flat!")

In fact it was rather difficult
for her to keep in her place
while she made her speech:
the two Queens pushed her so,
one on each side,
that they nearly lifted her up
into the air:
"I rise to return thanks—"
Alice began:
and she really did rise
as she spoke, several inches;
but she got hold
of the edge of the table,
and managed
to pull herself down again.

"Take care of yourself!"
screamed the White Queen,
seizing Alice's hair
with both her hands.
"Something's going to happen!"

And then
(as Alice afterwards described it)
all sorts of things happened
in a moment. The candles
all grew up to the ceiling,
looking something
like a bed of rushes
with fireworks at the top.
As to the bottles,
they each took a pair of plates,
which they hastily
fitted on as wings, and so,
with forks for legs,
went fluttering about
in all directions:

"and very like birds they look,"
Alice thought to herself,
as well as she could
in the dreadful confusion
that was beginning.

At this moment she heard
a hoarse laugh at her side,
and turned to see what was
the matter with the White Queen;
but, instead of the Queen,
there was the leg of mutton
sitting in the chair.
"Here I am!" cried a voice
from the soup tureen,
and Alice turned again,
just in time to see
the Queen's broad
good-natured face grinning at her
for a moment over the edge
of the tureen,
before she disappeared
into the soup.

There was not
a moment to be lost.
Already several of the guests
were lying down in the dishes,
and the soup ladle
was walking up the table
towards Alice's chair,
and beckoning to her
impatiently to get out of its way.

"I can't stand this any longer!"
she cried as she jumped up
and seized the table-cloth
with both hands: one good pull,
and plates, dishes, guests,
and candles came crashing down
together in a heap on the floor.

"And as for you," she went on,
turning fiercely

upon the Red Queen,
whom she considered
as the cause of all the mischief—
but the Queen
was no longer at her side—
she had suddenly
dwindled down to the size
of a little doll,
and was now on the table,
merrily running round and round
after her own shawl,
which was trailing behind her.

At any other time, Alice
would have felt surprised at this,
but she was far too much excited
to be surprised at anything now .
"As for you," she repeated,
catching hold of the little creature
in the very act of jumping over
a bottle which had just lighted
upon the table,
"I'll shake you into a kitten,
that I will!"

CHAPTER X.

Shaking

She took her
off the table as she spoke,
and shook her backwards
and forwards with all her might.

The Red Queen
made no resistance whatever;
only her face grew very small,
and her eyes got large and green:
and still,
as Alice went on shaking her,
she kept on growing shorter—
and fatter—and softer—
and rounder—and—

CHAPTER XI.

Waking

—and it really was a kitten,
after all.

CHAPTER XII.

Which Dreamed it?

"Your majesty
shouldn't purr so loud,"
Alice said, rubbing her eyes,
and addressing the kitten,
respectfully,
yet with some severity.
"You woke me out of oh!
such a nice dream!
And you've been along with me,
Kitty— all through
the Looking-Glass world.
Did you know it, dear?"

It is a very inconvenient habit
of kittens
(Alice had once made the remark)
that, whatever you say to them,
they always purr.
"If they would only purr for 'yes'
and mew for 'no,'
or any rule of that sort,"
she had said, "so that one could
keep up a conversation!
But how can you talk
with a person if they always
say the same thing?"

On this occasion the kitten
only purred:
and it was impossible to guess
whether it meant "yes" or "no."

So Alice hunted
among the chessmen on the table
till she had found the Red Queen:
then she went down on her knees
on the hearth-rug,
and put the kitten and the Queen
to look at each other.
"Now, Kitty!" she cried,
clapping her hands triumphantly.
"Confess that was
what you turned into!"

("But it wouldn't look at it,"
she said,
when she was explaining
the thing afterwards to her sister:
"it turned away its head,
and pretended not to see it:
but it looked
a little ashamed of itself,
so I think it must have been
the Red Queen.")

"Sit up a little more stiffly, dear!"
Alice cried with a merry laugh.
"And curtsey
while you're thinking
what to—what to purr.
It saves time, remember!"
And she caught it up
and gave it one little kiss,
"just in honour
of having been a Red Queen."

"Snowdrop, my pet!"
she went on,
looking over her shoulder
at the White Kitten,
which was still patiently
undergoing its toilet,
"when will Dinah have finished
with your White Majesty,
I wonder?
That must be the reason

you were so untidy
in my dream—Dinah!
do you know
that you're scrubbing
a White Queen? Really,
it's most disrespectful of you!

"And what did Dinah turn to,
I wonder?" she prattled on,
as she settled comfortably down,
with one elbow in the rug,
and her chin in her hand,
to watch the kittens.
"Tell me, Dinah, did you turn
to Humpty Dumpty?
I think you did—however,
you'd better not mention it
to your friends just yet,
for I'm not sure.

"By the way, Kitty,
if only you'd been really with me
in my dream, there was one thing
you would have enjoyed—
I had such a quantity of poetry
said to me, all about fishes!
To-morrow morning
you shall have a real treat.
All the time you're eating
your breakfast, I'll repeat
'The Walrus and the Carpenter'
to you;
and then you can make believe
it's oysters, dear!

"Now, Kitty,
let's consider who it was
that dreamed it all.
This is a serious question,
my dear,
and you should not go on
licking your paw like that—
as if Dinah hadn't
washed you this morning!

You see, Kitty, it must have been
either me or the Red King.
He was part of my dream,
of course—
but then I was part of his dream,
too! Was it the Red King, Kitty?
You were his wife, my dear,
so you ought to know—Oh,
Kitty, do help to settle it!
I'm sure your paw can wait!"
But the provoking kitten
only began on the other paw,
and pretended it hadn't heard
the question.

Which do you think it was?

A boat beneath a sunny sky,

Lingering onward dreamily
In an evening of July—

Children three that nestle near,

Eager eye and willing ear,

Pleased a simple tale to hear—

Long has paled that sunny sky:

Echoes fade and memories die.

Autumn frosts have slain July.

Still she haunts me,
phantomwise,

Alice moving under skies
Never seen by waking eyes.

Children yet, the tale to hear,

Eager eye and willing ear,

Lovingly shall nestle near.

In a Wonderland they lie,

Dreaming as the days go by,

Dreaming as the summers die:

Ever drifting down the stream—
Lingering in the golden gleam—
Life, what is it but a dream?

THE END